CONTENTS

Title Page
Copyright
Prologue — 1
Sixteen — 4
Twenty-five — 7
Brotherhood — 10
Tall, Dark and Handsome — 15
Mum and Dad — 20
Sisterhood — 26
Steve McQueen — 33
Trust — 38
Hey There, Michael! — 43
Housemate — 49
Lucky — 53
Bring The Kids — 76
Help me, Obi Wan — 92
Lidl — 98
Minefield — 102
Unforgivable — 107

Role Models	114
A Sort of Addiction	119
Dreams	124
Smirk	128
This One	132
A Cat is Just a Cat	141
It's Not Working	146
Bogs and Ducks	151
Going Potty	157
Mum and Dad's	161
Saturday	170
Ben's Flat	177
It's Over	183
Day of the Panther	187
Love, Part I	195
Love, Part II	200
Fast Car	204

BRING THE KIDS

Ellie Tennant

Copyright © 2023 Ellie Tennant

All rights reserved

The characters in this book are fictional, and any similarity to real persons, if not entirely coincidental, should not be taken as in any way an accurate representation.

No part of this book may be reproduced, or stored in a retrieval system, or transmitted in any form or by any means, electronic, mechanical, photocopying, recording, or otherwise, without express written permission of the publisher.

ISBN: 9798853752634

PROLOGUE

There was this bloke, this writer, and he was crap. He isn't the person this story is going to be about, this is just a kind of a warm-up, okay?
But this is all true as well.
Honestly, it's all going to be true. Well, as true as I can make it. Obviously, I'm not the memory man or anything, some of it might be vaguely inaccurate, but cut me some slack. I'm about to lay my innermost thoughts and feelings bare for you, the least you could do is not start doubting me on the first page.
You're investing a good few hours of your life in reading this, I don't want you to feel it was wasted. I'm not about to start making stuff up, I'm really trying to tell you something.
Maybe, I don't know, it'll ring a few bells with you, and you can think 'well, thank God I'm not the only one', and then the purpose of creative endeavour will be satisfied.
What is the purpose of creative endeavour?
Oh, I don't know. Think about it. Communication, I suppose. Telling other human beings 'hey, look, we're all people here, we're all doing this crazy stuff, why feel alone about it, eh?'
That's what cave paintings were about, I reckon. Cavemen could look at that and think 'well, thank Christ I'm not the only arsehole who spends all day trying to spear a sabre

toothed tiger before coming home with a bloody rabbit'. They'd feel less alone. They'd know there were other cavemen out there, hairy, ugly, all with huge jaw-bones jutting out and terminally crap at hunting.

I have got quite a big jaw bone myself, actually, but that's not what I feel the need to communicate about at this present time. I'm resigned to it. Shut up about it.

There are some scientists who believe that cave paintings may have just been a kind of prehistoric grafitti, but so what? What's grafitti if it's not some poor, disaffected, angry youth reaching out to other poor disaffected angry youths, just to feel less alone in the world?

Alright, so they may be reaching out to say 'fuck off, this is our poor disaffected neighbourhood, go and work out your destructive, directionless rage against society somewhere else' but they're still communicating. They want to be heard. They want someone to know how they feel. They want someone to know they woz here, so to speak.

So there was this bloke, the one the story's not about, but he's still relevant. At least, he is for this bit. He was a writer, and he was rubbish, I was reading about him only the other day.

He wrote spy stories, adventure stories, big action stories about big tough action heroes having spy adventures. Sounds great doesn't it? It wasn't.

The truth was he was forty, and he lived with his Mum. He'd never been married, he'd never even had a girlfriend. This is a bit like one of those cavemen doing a load of chalk paintings about being an astronaut. It just wouldn't wash, none of the other cavemen would have believed it. 'You're a spear-chucking hunter-gatherer' they would have shouted at him, just deal with it.

This man, this poor writing failure, he stayed at home and lived life through his writing for twenty years. This sounds poetic, but judging by how crap people thought his writing was, it was just a tragic waste of time.

Not one story or book or poem he ever, ever wrote got published, or even read by anybody other than his Mum. Except the publishers, who thought it was crap. It was crap. Sad bastard.

Then one day, one of his (presumably) very few friends suggested he wrote about something he actually knew something about.

'You're a useless, appalling bloody failure, mate' they would have said, stirring his pot noodle for

him with a biro, 'You need to start writing about something else. Write about something you know about, for God's sake.'

'But the only thing I know anything about is being an appalling useless bloody failure,' our hero would have protested.

'So write about that then' his friend would have said, popping the biro back in his hand and passing him a wad of clean A4. 'Write about a man who is crap at everything. Go on, it'll be a laugh'

So he did.

It became one of the single most successful sitcoms in British television history.

What was it?
Oh, I'll tell you at the end. That's a true story, by the way. And this is a true story too.

SIXTEEN

When I was sixteen someone stole my face. One day I looked in the mirror and I realised it was a different shape. I don't know how familiar you are with the effects of hundreds and hundreds of spots on the human face, so I will try to explain it to you. Not as a text-book, or a doctor would, but actually explain it to you, how it feels to live under there.
There's a myth that Eskimos have a hundred different words for snow.
No, I know they don't.
But you can imagine why they might. You know, they wake up, look out of the window.
'Mummy, mummy! It's snowing!' Of course they bloody don't. It's everywhere, all the time. They drive through it, dig through it, look at it, and no doubt get completely pissed off with it.
Bloody snow. Powdery snow, deep snow, sludgy snow, the sort of snow that gets right through sealskin and ruins the fluffy interior of your boots. Basically, there's a lot of it about.
It's a bit like that with spots. You learn to recognise the different types.
The little white heads, ones that are white as soon as they appear, they're no trouble. Passive little beggars, they hang around for maybe three days, then fall off

sheepishly, probably regretting bothering in the first place.

Little red ones, more painful, still bearable. Unless you badger them and badger them with toilet paper and finger nails. Then the top will go weepy and you will have a small hot tub of nasty watery wetness on your forehead for a week.

Big painful lumps, like marbles under the skin, which never come to a head. These will make your eyes water every time you change expression and pulsate quietly to your own gentle internal rhythms.

When I was sixteen, when my face was not my own, I had hundreds of those.

The Ray Winston of the acne world, a big rock-hard cockney bastard of a spot. A spot, no doubt, who started life training to be a hod-carrier but decided to become a great big fucking rock-hard boil for a career instead. Toothpaste does not have a noticeable effect on these spots — I cannot , claim a knowledge of whether it works on Ray Winston.

The thing nobody ever talks about is the pain. Like childbirth, the pain of having acne is shrouded in mystery and carefully woven lies. As if it's bad enough we should have to look at it, without the poor bugger on the receiving end moaning about how his chin feels like it's been dipped in scalding tea before being savaged by a thousand furious tea-loving hornets. It hurts. It really hurts.

One thing which alleviates the pain very slightly is to get rid of the poison, not always possible on the stubborn ones, but it makes smiling less of an agonising chore. Hence the squeezing.

Why do some people get acne and not others? I don't

know. The one group of people who are immune by nature from getting skin blemishes of any kind are the new partners of your ex-boyfriend. They will, as dictated by the delicate biorhythms of biology and human nature and sod's law, have skin like sand-blasted alabaster. Of course they will.
So there I was at sixteen, in the bathroom. No, it's just a bathroom. I'm not going through all this again, just picture it, bath, sink, you know the score.
I was looking in the mirrored door of the small medicine cabinet of the sink.
My nose was bulging on either side with red boils.
Who did this to me?
Unfortunately for my non-immortal soul I am an atheist, otherwise I could probably have blamed God and taken it as a sign to change my ways and would probably by now be Mother 'walnut in a blanket' Theresa. I have problems with God. I can only presume, given my run of luck in life, that he feels the same way about me. It's just the starving Africans, what about the starving Africans? I mean, why would he do that? What's he trying to prove? Okay, okay, I know there's plenty of food and we have to learn to re-distribute it and all that stuff, I know that. But why pray to the bastard to mend old Nannie's leg if he's just let a tiny African shit out her own intestines due to chronic malnutrition? What's his door policy?
I know you might feel 'starving Africans' to be somewhat passé. Passé to us maybe. Presumably to them thinking 'oh fuck, oh fuck, I've got no fucking dinner' every night until they die painfully and prematurely, they are more wont to feel the pressurised immediacy of the issue.
So no, thank you for asking, I don't do God.

TWENTY-FIVE

Let's fast forward a few years. Not too many years, not to now. Not that far. Put the brakes on a bit. Go forward about nine years. I'm about twenty five now. Got a degree in English, blonde hair, young.....looking good?
Not a bit of it.
This is all true, I promise you. I want to actually convey something meaningful here, you know. This isn't just creative masturbation. I want you to know all this for a reason. Stay with me, it's a good story, and there will be sex in it.

The spots came back.
Having once had acne in one's youth is a bit like the fat woman who loses loads of weight but can't stop going into fat people's shops. I read about that once in a magazine, I've never been fat myself. Once you've had it, it never leaves you. You become addicted to your rituals, your cleansing products, hanging them on your face like garlic to keep the vampires away.
It's got it's plus side, of course. People who have never had their faces stolen from them take them somewhat for granted, I often feel. They probably don't run their fingertips over their smooth foreheads relishing the feel of their own skin, or tilt their heads at an angle in

the light to appreciate the unimpeded contours of their cheek. It's not vanity, with me. Honestly. Come on, you've come this far with me, you know that now. It's partly wonder, partly joy. But that's now, the now now, not when I was twenty five.

The spots came back.

The spots did go for a while in my early twenties. It was like the best present in the world …. ..and what's under the tree this year?

Why, it's only my FUCKING FACE. Thank you. I thought maybe acne was like mumps, you could only get it once and then not worry about it ever again. It turns out it's more like depression — you spend your whole life wondering when another attack will come and leave you whimpering under a duvet for the next six months.

And when I was twenty five, it was back.

It was the year that somebody shot Jill Dando, I was twenty-five then. That was also the time when my Dad was buying me the Radio Times every week, in the apparent hope that somewhere therein would lie the answer to all my problems.

That week, the week that somebody shot Jill Dando, she was on the front cover of the Radio Times.

There was also an advert on the back for a bookclub, and the heading of the advert was 'MURDER'.

I'm not kidding. Fate is a bastard sometimes. I kept that issue, because I thought there was some meaning in there somewhere, if only I knew what it was. Weird stuff happens sometimes and it seems like, I don't know, it should mean something. Like the time I saw a peacock outside the ladies toilets in the carpark behind the cinema. It's as if fate, in an unusually benevolent mood, was saying, 'Hey, you've had enough of this shit. Here, have a peacock. That'll cheer you up'.

So, there I was. A mid-twenties Radio Times reader. Let's talk about it in the present tense, it'll make it feel as if it's actually happening.

So here I am. I'm a single Mum. Lonely, obviously, distraught with grief and anger at a terrible betrayal, but let's not go on about that now.

I have two boys, toddlers, and haven't had any other love in my life for over a year.

BROTHERHOOD

Here is my friend, Phil. She's great isn't she? We are in my house getting ready to go to her house for lunch and the stress components are mounting by the second. Joining hands in a great daisy chain of stress, dancing merrily across the tortured landscape of my own head.
The kids, the kids are stressful. I have to get ready and I can't.
No, I can't even start to get ready because I can't even look at my own face.
'It would help if you cleaned the mirror occasionally' Phil tells me, watching me grimacing at my reflection.
'I want to look nice' I tell her. No, forget that. 'I just want to look alright. I want to forget about my face completely, not be reminded every second of it by the throbbing pain of the poison under my bloody skin.'
It's the Ray Winston ones, remember? The boils. Christ to God, it hurts like hell.
I want to look alright because here's the clincher. Phil has a brother.
When you're a single Mum you don't meet people. The woman in the Co-op, maybe. Or the couple who run the toddler group in the local church, but not people like this. I met him two weeks ago and here I am about to meet him again and my face has the texture of porridge. Ready Brek, I could handle.
Phil takes charge. She's over six foot is Phil, and she can

take charge. She takes charge in a nice way, not that way women sometimes do, effecting bolshy bossiness to indicate self-conscious concern. Not a 'now this is for your own good' kind of taking charge. Not an attempt to conceal their own personal inadequacies by affecting to cure everyone else's. Not that. More of a 'shall I take charge, as you appear to be flidding out quite considerably' kind of taking charge. Nice.

She sits me down and tells me the truth. Again, let me qualify that, in case you get the wrong impression of Phil. She doesn't tell women who look like shit the truth to score cheap points. She told me the truth because she was dealing with it, sorting it out, and bloody well getting stuff done. Good girl Phil.

I am crying now. It's not vanity, I swear to God, it's not vanity. Not wanting to feel agonisingly hideous is not vanity.

'My face looks like a bowl of breakfast cereal' I say.

'You can't even see what you look like yet' she points out. The mirror is pretty dirty, my eighteen- hour days filled with infant faeces and teletubby videos do not yet offer me any windows for extraneous activities. Like cleaning. Or eating. I could clean during the teletubby video, you say? Well I could, but those things are hypnotic. The bright colours, the barely distinguishable words, it lulls you.

'Look, I'll do your face.' says Phil.

'Will you cover up the boils?'

'They're not boils, they're spots.' she says, silencing my protests with some good old-fashioned mumsie common-sense. No nonsense, no mucking about. That's Phil.

'Have you got another one of these cover sticks? We're

going to need quite a lot.'
'Just put a bag over my head and get it over with'
'Do you want me to do this or don't you?
'I don't want to have fucking boils'
'Spots'
'I feel disgusting'
'You don't look disgusting. You look like someone who has spots.'
Nobody has ever told me the truth about my skin before. People say 'oh, it doesn't show' and then you never trust them again.
But what else could they say?
Talking of trust, I read about this woman once, who'd been in Auschwitz. She said one of the things it left her with was a way of classifying people. She'd look at people and know, immediately, would they have risked their lives to give her a bit of bread?
She said she could see it, straight away, which those people were.
I classify people. Not like that, obviously, I've never had to cope with anything like that. But I classify people, as far as the retardation of my own limited life experience will allow. Usually I put them in 'brotherhood' or 'thought police'. Are they one of us? Are they secretly like us, secretly disagreeing with everything and angry about everything but trying to look normal?
Or have they got one eye on their greasy pole, no social conscience, and would shop you to big brother the first time you twitched in church? Bastards.
There's quite a few like that. You can tell a subversive thought has never crossed their well-conditioned minds. They quack the duckspeak, put their unobtrusive toe on the party lines, there's no well-hidden rebellion.

Sometimes you meet one of us.

Someone who is talking rather than quacking. Oh come on, read the book, then you'll know.

I'm cross-referencing here, assuming knowledge on the part of the reader.

For Christ's sake, it's the oldest literary convention in the book. Deal with it.

'1984' by George Orwell, I'm talking about.

Well, whatever. People like us, you and me.

'When you squeeze them, it makes them go weepy and they're impossible to cover up' she says, irritably. I don't think she's that irritated, it would be pretty unkind to be irritated by someone else's acne. Like people who sigh when wheelchair users block up a corridor a bit. Yeah, sure, it'll take you thirty extra seconds to get down the corridor, but what's that compared to being able to take yourself for a shit on your own, eh? Have some compassion, for Christ's sake.

'I want to get rid of them' I say. I've surrendered to petulance, now I'm being looked after. It feels nice. 'Stop eating chocolate' she says bluntly. She's a bored of this, I can tell. But I can be a terrier on some subjects. I don't let go until it's dead.

'It's got nothing to do with chocolate. I've picked them until my face is one huge weeping sore. Then that makes me so unhappy I pick them even more. Now I look like an outpatient at a fucking burns unit'.

'Well then, leave them a-fucking-lone'.

Maybe she is a bit irritable. 'If my face looked like that I'd be upset too' she assures me, with that beautiful jarring honesty which has lost her friends all over the country. She's trying to be nice, swallowing her irritation at my outbursts and my petulance. I appreciate it.

She leans over me to inspect it, she smells nice. I'm very sensitive to smell. I once went to see 'Johnny Handsome' with Mickey Rourke, years ago, and I was sitting behind a man who stank. He really stank, unwashed nasty man stink, you know the one. As luck would have it, 'Johnny Handsome' is a dark and brooding affair concerning an ugly man's seedy, and presumably smelly, existence. I can't remember any more than that. That terrible smell in the seat in front of us lent the film an ambience and a touch of realism that it surely could never have had if you rented out and watched it sitting next to your glade plug-in. It was like a total sensory experience. Thank you, smelly man, whoever you were.
Phil smells nice, it makes her honesty easier to bear. The sugar spoonful.
'Your skin has a texture to it, I can't change that. But I can make it all one colour. It won't look perfect, but it'll look okay. Shall I do that?'
I can go from looking like the singing detective without his foundation on to looking okay, without even getting up? Without sobbing and patting and squeezing for twenty desperate minutes? She is so kind and gentle, my friend who smells nice, like an acne nurse. A cosmetic paramedic. So here I am, covered up and coloured in like a minstrel in reverse.
Like I've mixed rice-crispies in flour and sneezed into it.
Don't laugh, I'm about to go and see the man of my dreams, remember? There, that sobered you up.

TALL, DARK AND HANDSOME

Maybe it's not enough just to know that his sister smells nice and deals with stuff. I will try to describe him.
He's tall.
Don't think 'tall' in terms of anyone you know. Think 'bloody, bloody tall' in terms of the tallest person you can think of, and then add some. Add a lot. He's bloody tall. He's six feet seven inches tall, and that's pretty damn tall by anyone's standards.
Maybe you're thinking, well, its pointless trying to describe his face if he's that tall isn't it? I mean, all you'd ever do is stare up his nostrils anyway.
Don't be bloody stupid. He sits down, you see it.
He's clever, too. I met him for the first time last week, you see. He's got 'brotherhood' written all over him. The thought police would have a field day with this guy, he's a genuine mental subversive. He turned off the telly when we all went over there, actually turned it off, and said, 'It'll feel weird for the first ten minutes, but when we get used to the silences, we'll start to have a conversation.'
That hooked me in.
I can't stand it when people's eyes drift lazily over to electronic stimuli while you're trying to engage them in conversation. Human contact and interaction is the

cornerstone of a healthy psyche, just look at people who do round the world yacht racing. Take away your conversation and that's it, you're wrapped in a cagoule with the string tied under your chin and eating dried stuff out of packets with chapped fingertips. Don't do it, man. Connect with people.
Chuckling indulgently at your text messages while some poor sod stares at the top of your head, is also unforgivable. Other people's text messages are like anecdotes about drunken escapades when you were eighteen; they are interesting only to yourself and the shiny-faced self-indulgent wankers you shared them with; I do not care for them.
I wonder if primitive cave people got pissed off when some of their number began scribbling evasively all over the walls during an in-depth grunt about mammoth tusks.
'Oh look,' they said to themselves, 'I'm trying to use a fledgling form of primitive speech to convey a simple narrative about hunting, and that cunt is just communicating with future, more sophisticated generations. Can't he put his chalk on silent just for one evening?"
I can't stand it.
So he did, he hooked me in.
So you've got tall, good, that's the first bit. Big brown eyes, he's got those, with a white mole over his right eyebrow. I notice things like that, small bumps and imperfections, I like them. They give the eye a focal point, something to focus on. I know this woman with the smoothest face I've ever seen, completely smooth and — here's the bit that'll freak you out — the same colour as her hair. I'm probably just imagining it, but I would swear her clothes were that

colour too, a beigy, pinky sort of colour, like an anaemic baby gerbil. Your eyes sort of slide off her as if your vision was a greased baby trying to sit in a high chair made of butter. I can't picture her, my eyeline cannot maintain contact with hers for long enough to form any sort of impression.
He's got full lips, I like full lips. He looks a bit like Elvis when he smiles, something to do with the way the cheeks curve, I think. Will Smith has that too. Honestly, look at his cheeks.
His name's Danny, a nice sensible name.
I met him last week and he thought I was pretty. That burns through my self-hatred a bit. I could, at a stretch, be described as pretty, when I'm not covered in boils. Or when, as in this case, my boils are concealed by foundation and can only make their presence felt by lumping and bumping the surface of my face and aching if I inadvertently flare my nostrils.
It is hard to convey just how completely acne hijacks your every experience. It's like looking at life through acne-coloured glasses, everything you do you experience in terms of your acne.
I think gay people feel a bit like that, they go to the cinema, turn on the telly, where are the people like them? Where are their role models, the ones they can relate to, doing brave and sexy and enviable things with their worthwhile and enviable lives? There are some, yes, specifically about being gay.
Well done Mr. Entertaimnent and his all-encompassing arms.
But for acne sufferers, spotty bastards, pizza-faces, call us what you will, there are none.
There are no films where the spotty bastard gets the man

(or the girl). Unthinkable, isn't it?

Where were we? Oh yes, Phil is taking me to her house for lunch. Her brother will be there, man of dreams, it's all coming back to you now, isn't it?

My children's father arrives to collect them, he's taking them out for the day. This, according to the British legal system as it currently stands, makes him Mary fucking Poppins and legally allowed to do or fuck whatever he likes as long as he doesn't do it to the children.

His wife? Well, bollocks to her. She knew the risks when she took the job.

Sorry, fathers for Justice, but put away your batman suits for a minute and think about it properly. Quite often, 'She's using the children against me' just means 'Look, I want to screw women younger than her and run about for most of the week pleasing myself while she is driven to white-knuckle madness at the hands of our two-year-old, and still pop my head up every now and then to play Mary Poppins for a weekend. I'll even get the young slapper I sacrificed my marriage for to jump off my cock for half an hour, how about it?'

Strangely, when faced with the possibility of some philandering tosser having everything in the way of freedom, sex and not having to get up and clean puke off the ladder of the bunk beds at four in the morning, and having their children as well, some women balk. They've been up since five-thirty watching a two-foot high miniature version of the bastard spray their lounge with coco-pops, exactly how reasonable do you expect them to be?

Addled with betrayal, exhaustion, loneliness and a simple desire to just sit down with a cup of fucking tea, for crying out loud, women get nasty. And no wonder.

Get that expression off your face, Batman, climb down fiom your telegraph pole, and offer to have the kids every other night. If your girlfriend wouldn't like that, if it wouldn't fit in with your lifestyle, you can fuck off. Get a cat.

Their father comes to the door. I don't want him to see me looking like shit. I don't want him to think, 'Thank God I ditched that spotty cow and got in a younger model.' I want him to ache with longing and memory, of course I do. I want him to regret the day he moved in with a teenage girl with big tits and burn with the golden memories of our love. But he doesn't. He gets the kids and fucks off.

Briefly, shakily, exhaustedly, I'm free.

Like the old man let out of his shackles and shuffling blinking into the sunlight, I get into Phil's car.

MUM AND DAD

I am at my parent's house, drinking tea on the patio.
What?
Oh, that. Yeah, that went okay. He was there, we had what your Mum would describe as a nice chat. He said he would ring, but he hasn't.
I was trying not to think about it actually, thanks for reminding me. That was two months ago. The whole 'man of dreams' stuff, I feel a bit embarrassed about that now. My parents keep asking about him. 'That tall man you liked,' they call him. It's hard, sometimes, the way your parents seem to gauge the effectiveness of their parenting skills on the quality of the sexual partner you are able to attract. My Dad leapt upon the information that Danny worked at a university with the fervour of a medieval priest at a witch-hunt. A university? Clever? Good gene pool? It must be an animal thing.
A hang-over from that whole survival of the fittest mentality. Give me survival of the nicest any day of the week. If nature dictates that Goebbels is more deserving of longevity than Stephen Hawking, I resign. I do, I fucking resign from the human race.
Anyway, here's my Dad. Tightly rolled shirt-sleeves, tightly pulled up socks, big Adam's apple and an expression which clearly says 'when you've been here as long as I have, your Adam's apple will look like that too'.
He's a bit uptight, my Dad. Probably because my Mum

has told him to bollock off every morning for forty years. He's holding his tea tightly because he has one of my toddlers on his knee. Toddler in one hand, fag and tea in the other. Only granddads can do that and not look like a social worker's bread and butter. My Dad looks like those photos taken in the forties, where fags and tightly rolled up shirtsleeves were no bar to being perceived as a decent person.
He puts his tea down, absolutely centrally in the middle of the table. Honestly. Then he touches the handle gently so it points in the right direction. Nobody knows what the right direction is except Dad, and he isn't telling. He looks like he knows what he's doing, though. Like he's got a sort of bigger plan.
I'm telling my Mum about my acne.
'Don't squeeze it,' she says. 'They don't really show that much anyway'.
She's not that interested, I can tell. She's playing patience at the kitchen table really quickly. And I mean really quickly. Faster than anyone ever should be able to play it. The cards slap slap slap in time to her over-active but utterly unfocussed mind. She's like one of those wind-up teeth things, my Mum. There's loads going on, loads of momentum there, but it doesn't seem to have any real direction. Eventually the kids get bored with it and it just leaps pointlessly off the table. The teeth thing, I mean, not my Mum.
When I was a kid she played mind games incessantly. Not that kind of mind game, not deliberately winding people up with subtle manipulation in order to confuse and disorientate them, not that sort of mind game. Real mind games. Like 'Countdown', and a little battery-run thing that beeped — and, for one strange and half-remembered

summer, the computer game Chucky Egg. Her fingers battered the battery thing so much all the numbers wore off and she could still do it from memory. What was it? Christ, I don't know. Some numbers thing, you had to add up all the numbers before it went beep or something. God knows. She could do it faster than you could tap the William Tell overture on the cover of this book. Try it. Nope, she was faster.

There is a theory that all the energy in the universe is simply in circulation, continuously repeating itself in an eternal cycle in which there is no creation and no destruction. The circular nature of the Earth mirrored in the circular nature of energy and the very universe itself. That's my Mum.

Sometimes I wonder what would happen if she actually harnessed all that energy, if we strapped her to a treadmill or something. She could strap herself into the national grid and tap out enough beeping stuff to power all the plug sockets in the country for fifty years.

As it is, she doesn't know what to do with it. It comes out as temper sometimes. Okay, a lot of times. 'BOLLOCK OFF' See, told you.

She's talking to my Dad. He's defrosting a Wall's Vienetta in a way which contradicts the legal guidelines. Her legal guidelines, not Wall's. They don't give a shit any more, we've bought the fucking thing, their input in the matter is finished as far as they're concerned. .

'So, any news on this tall man you liked?' My Dad wants me to get married. He wants the kids to have a stable, loving, traditional family home to be sure, but he also wants someone else to be responsible for supplying them with Wall's Vienetta.

The tall man hasn't phoned.

He hasn't phoned.
I look like shit.
'He was really nice, Dad. He worked at the university'
'Good, good'.

Dad's face is arranged at right angles to his peace of mind. Adam's apple, jaw line, brow furrow, all perfectly lined up. I want to please him because I always want to please him, I just want to soften up those right angles a bit. When I talk to my Dad I'm always eleven. Asking to go out on my brother's old Grifter bike and knowing he'll worry about me. Shit, the past is like a fucking skewer sometimes. A skewer that's already been in the chicken, greasy with time.
I look like shit.
'So has he phoned you up?'
'No.'
'He's not the right man for you then, is he?'
Dad speaks quickly when he says things like this, makes announcements about the state of life in the world today. Things that are true to any right-thinking person with a backbone, moral fibre, and a bloody good British jaw-line. My parent's dog is in the way, shedding white hairs over piles of blankets. Why do your Mum and Dad stockpile big blankets? Is it a war thing? We'll need those blankets in a hurry if the sirens go off. Relax guys, no-one's had to sit outside under corrugated iron while the Luftewaffe carpets the skies for fifty years.
The dog is fat in a lumpy kind of way. She has bits kind sticking out of her as if she was badly made out of play doh the night Tony Hart got pissed and ran amok in TV centre, just having a laugh. The dog's name is Florin, which is a reference to my parent's previous lumpy ancient dog. Previous lumpy dog had four puppies, all

named after old money.
Penny, Tanner, Bob, old money, apparently. You've got parents, they'll tell you.
The first thing your Dad remembers is something that 'cost him two bob'. Ask him, go on. Well, that's my Dad too.
They like circular stuff, my Mum and Dad. Stuff that seems to be connected to other stuff and makes sense. Family names, you know.
I suppose atheists have to find their own reasons for things, reasons that make you feel like everything did have a point to it after all. Like life isn't just loads of random shit, spraying out senselessly all over eternity, it had a reason and a resonance. Calling your dog Florin because the other ones had names like Tuppence gives things a bit of resonance. A bit of continuity. Throwing a totally unexpected 'Rover' into the mix could seriously screw up my Mum and Dad's ripples in the delicate time line of infinity.
'My back is killing me. Really killing me.' My Mum's fingers don't pause, independently slapping and slicing and deciding in a game of cards she doesn't appear to be involved in.
'Bending down to pick up the ball for the bloody dog. Bloody killing me.'
'That tall man didn't phone me, Mum.' I want her to know but I also want it to be words — I want it to exist somehow. When I was a kid, Mum was sometimes too wrapped up in her beeping games to really listen. She could solve your peer pressure problems without looking up from adding up numbers really fucking fast. Beep. Well done.
'Who's this tall man then?'

Okay, sometimes she does listen. She's alright, my Mum.
The dog looks up at me beseechingly. They all look beseeching, don't they? What do her eyes tell me? 'I can understand your emotions faster than you can, I have an instinctive knowledge about life borne from centuries of surviving on instinct.'
'Peter,' says my Mum, 'The bloody dog needs a shit again'.
The tall man hasn't phoned.

SISTERHOOD

I am at home, sharing the same space and time with my housemate, Gemma. That's as far as any similarity goes. My Dad gave me a lift home because, as I've already told you, when I'm around him I'm still only eleven. I'm in my house now, the kids are in bed, and I've managed to recoup those fifteen years since my Dad dropped me off.
Here's Gemma, she always looks like that. She's bloody miserable, just a complete bloody misery with a centre parting and slightly bad breath. Not very bad breath — that would be verging on being interesting. She told me she was on Prozac last year with depression.
She is sitting here now, eating dry toast, staring at me. She stares at me, Gemma does, waiting for me to have a personality so she doesn't have to put the effort in. Occasionally she disagrees with me, just to show that she's actually a contentiously fascinating individual in her own right. She's not, she's disagreeing with me for the sake of it. This makes me hate her more than it should.
So that's Gemma, Prozac, dry food, dry hair. Do you know what picture she's got on her bedroom door? Guess, go on, I want you to.
Little Miss Sunshine.
For Christ's sake!
She comes alive in ront of men, I've noticed that. When I say men, I mean men she might want to sleep with. The dry toast, the Prozac, that doesn't get a look in.

Even her parting looks a little less central somehow. All this doesn't mean that she does actually become more interesting, she just throws out feelers which give the impression she might be interesting, were they grounded in anything approaching reality. Phil heard her telling a man that she'd always wanted to go travelling, at a party last week. Travelling, Gemma? What, inspired by a sense of awe at the grotesque yet ultimately beautiful size of the universe in comparison with our own tiny and insignificant selves? No, just firing off a couple of clichés in the hope they might solidify into a real person.
No chance.
She eats dry cereal as well. Who the hell eats dry cereal? Except Americans, obviously. I'm not talking about eating it out of the packet dry, sitting in front of an episode of 'Rosanne' in a pair of baggy track suit bottoms, not that. Nothing that cool or transatlantic.
She puts it in a fucking bowl. A fucking bowl, and eats it dry with a spoon.
What sort of screwed-up bastardisation of a breakfast is that?
Washed down by a nice hot cup of milkless tea. Yes, you heard correctly. I can only presume that she is physically incapable of eating food which is more interesting than she is. And that prohibits pretty much everything.
I'm finding her more unbearable than usual tonight. It's a shallow reason, don't think badly of me. She's just come back from holiday, and her skin looks amazing. She is tanned, glowing, healthy, young, gorgeous, how many adjectives do you need? Bland, yes, dull and boring as my own shit, but who would know that to look at her tonight? I am in agony, and I despise her for the smallest things. Reaching up to scratch her face — a

casual gesture, one you'd hardly notice. If you have acne, you cannot scratch your face. Especially if that acne is 'concealed' with thick foundation, stifling your pores into such indignation they spew out some more acne, just to get you back.
You can't scratch your face. Scabby ones, ones you've picked and made them bleed, you'd make them bleed again, which is never attractive to the eye. Bulbous ones, ones full of poison that just won't come to a head, don't scratch those. It hurts. It bloody bloody hurts, and there's that cunt, that spotless, shining, gleamingly acne-free cunt, sitting there, scratching away like the last dog in Battersea Dog's Home.
I fucking hate her.
'I feel like shit,' I say, 'I feel really spotty tonight.'
I can't sit in silence, my resentment will climb up my windpipe and spell out my hatred in a big thought bubble over my head.
'Don't squeeze them' she says, some dry toast spraying over her pyjamas.
'It makes them worse.' Her eyes flick back to the documentary on the telly.
'They don't show anyway.'
Liar. Liar. Liar.
'Really? They're really not that bad?'
One thing I didn't explain; I really am that desperate to believe it. Even from her dusty desert of a mouth. I want to believe it so badly, I get her to say it again.
'They feel pretty bad'. Say it again, please. It might make it come true.
'Honestly, they don't show'.
I really am that desperate.
She is thought police, through and through. It is almost

as though she fears the ministry of acne is listening via a microphone secreted behind my John Waterhouse on the lounge wall. She quacks the duckspeak like a professional everyman. Don't worry, secret all-powerful omnipotent governing body, there's no original or subversive thought here. It's all as it should be, as anyone could predict it could be.

I'd just rather all this mediocrity wasn't eating dry toast in the middle of my fucking lounge.

How can I get her to move out? How would I cope without her rent? To me, she appears like a bundle of ten-pound notes in front of my eyes, in the same way live chickens sometimes appear as sandwiches to Scoobie Doo. She may be dull, but her rent pays for the Action Man trainers.

The fleas are leaping joyfully out of the carpet.

They really are happy, our fleas. It is a hot summer, a real inflamed anus of a season, hot sun, hot air, hot face. I think they're cat fleas, from a cat I used to have with the kids' Dad. A ginger thing with a bent tail, the cat, not their Dad, we called it 'Stockwell' after a stop on the Northern Line London tube.

When he went, he took it with him. I kept the boys. Fair trade. The cat would not have got me up six times a night until I wanted to headbutt myself unconscious on the kitchen cupboards, but then again, nor would it one day be old enough to bring me a degree of comfort and joy in my late middle-age. So, it's always that sort of trade-off with cats, isn't it?

It left me the fleas.

They celebrate the simplicity of their existence by jumping up momentarily into the air.

'Hurray! We're only fleas! The complexities of the human soul don't matter to us! Your miseries and heartbreaks are nothing to simple organisms who merely live and die and cannot contemplate the possible meanings thereof! What do we care? We're fucking fleas!'

We watch the documentary in silence, she disagrees with some of my observations about it a couple of times, so I shut up. Partly I shut up because I have a huge misshapen lip, due to an angry boil. It didn't start out angry, it was probably just a bit irritable when it first came up, but I have sat here for an hour pressing it and poking it and now, let me tell you, it's pissed off.

All this hatred hasn't just come out of nowhere, you know. It's not that unreasonable. While there's a bit of a quiet period where we're just watching telly, I'll explain it to you.

It's a long story, get comfy.

I mentioned I was a single Mum. Come on, you can't have missed it. The grandparents, the Action Man trainers. There's a reason why I'm a single Mum. That's why I'm lonely, distraught with grief and anger at a terrible betrayal, remember? I did mention it.

Yeah, well, Gemma's sort of involved in all of that. Not like that, not like you're thinking. She didn't sleep with the kid's Dad or anything. Her own involvement is more subtle than that, which makes it harder to throw her out. But easier to hate her. Hating when you don't know whether your hatred is justified burns far more scorchingly in the soul than hating a blatant arsehole. Be blatant, arseholes, and let us hate you without the soul barbeque, if you wouldn't mind.

When I say you don't know if your hatred is justified, I'm not talking about not knowing whether they've done the thing or not. That's easy, that's a piece of piss. Find out, then hate the bastard. It'll twist your personality into a

warped and ugly version of it's former light-hearted self, but it won't scorch your soul. Not like this.
What about, when you know they've done something. You know it. But is it really that bad? Is it
forgiveable? Shouldn't you just stop frothing at the mouth and get on with your life for a moment?
Is the effect it has on you in perfect balance with the badness of the actual thing? Are you, in short, just going a bit over the top. That girl you know from the restaurant didn't actually think it was that bad. But then, she wasn't there.
Betrayal is a terrible thing. It smells bad. Metaphorically, yes, it smells pretty bad that way, I'll grant you. But it actually smells bad, too.
Robert Winston did this documentary on the telly, this programme about smell. Apparently, we're more governed by our sense of smell than we realise. We sniff out our potential sex partners like well-practised labradors finding posh people's pheasants in the undergrowth. People with the opposite genetic make-up to our own smell sexier, which makes sense I suppose. Stops us from breeding with our brothers or sisters, unless you read the News of the World, in which case you'll believe everyone's doing that anyway. It also explains why mixed-race people are usually so good looking, spread those genes apart, it's what we're supposed to be doing.
So we've got all these senses which are all talking to us, we just never listen. Or we drown them out with intellectual processes or prejudices or other human weirdness. Except the smell thing, I'm listening to that, I'm sensitive to smell. Even before Professor Winston started sniffing the armpits of all those girl's tee-shirts, I listened to my

sense of smell. Except, now its been on the telly, who will believe me? Damn Robert Winston, give me back my breathtaking originality of thought, you pre-empting bastard.

So, smell.

Gemma smells bad. She smells wrong. Her breath, her feet, they're all wrong. That isn't the betrayal, of course. But it's a subtle betrayal, one I don't know if I can allow myself to hate her for. That girl I used to know from the restaurant, she thought I was a bit mad. But then, she wasn't there.

Still comfy?

STEVE MCQUEEN

His name was Tone. That's cockney for 'Anthony', but everyone called him Tone. He was my boys' Dad, he still is as it happens, but I'm going back in time a bit here. Let's not confuse the issue, I'll stick in the past tense for this bit.
I met him years ago, when I was young and gorgeous and still celebrating the fact my acne had cleared up. Hey, I didn't know it was going to come back. Here I am then, twenty one, blonde, skinny with the sheer exuberance of being young and gorgeous, and lined up on the runway of fate to meet 'Tone'.
Try to imagine Steve McQueen working as a British lorry driver. Do it. Take him off his motorbike, get him out of that barbed wire, and put him a lorry. Actually, it was a van, sorry, put him in a van. Company logo on the side, cheeky pair of tailored khaki shorts and three-button tee-shirt a size too small. You know the type.
I think something happens to good middle class girls when they leave university and are suddenly confronted by unadulterated masculinity. My boyfriends at university, they were the thinking types, obviously, they thought about stuff and analysed it all. That's very nice, but it doesn't build up the calf muscles. Tone wasn't the university type. He was pretty clever in an organic sort of unpolished way, but where I had previously looked for wit, I now saw tattoos. And, don't hate me for this, but

it made a change.

It was one of those sudden sex things, one of those nothing-but sex things, like suddenly getting a McDonald's after years of health food. He wasn't exactly vegetarian tofu, but bloody hell a couple of burgers can taste good. Unpretentiously good, like they're saying 'yeah, you can kiss goodbye to your arteries, but who needs 'em anyway?'. Devil-may-care, you know. Bad for you but who gives a fuck.

We met in a bar and made a date for the next night.

We kissed on the way home and what do you know? A year later we've moved in to my Mum and Dad's to save money because I'm pregnant.

Sorry, did I skip a bit there?

I'm just trying to move the story along a bit. Don't worry, Gemma and I are still watching telly, concentrate on this background bit for a minute.

So, where were we? We moved in with my Mum and Dad, we spent six months listening to my Mum telling us her back bloody hurts when she bends down to pick up the ball for the dog. Then we found a flat, then a little house. Perfect. Everything in order, like a game of Monopoly. Little houses on the board, buying stuff as you go around, very nice.

I had the first baby, that fucking hurt. Wait, hold on, let's not rush this story along too much, I'd like to dwell on this fact for a moment. It FUCKING HURT. Gas and air? That's like sniffing a marker pen to mask the pain of having your leg sawn off. Pethidine? The same thing, only they stab you in the arse with the marker pen. Next time you see your Mum, run up to her shouting 'How the living Christ did you do that?'. She'll weep tears of joy at your sudden realisation that your simple contribution to the great woven cloth of eternity was achieved at the expense of her fanny. She screamed her arse off, and she'd like you to apologise for that at least once, trust me. Epidurals, they're okay, they work. Why do women feel as if they have in some way 'failed' if they don't give birth with nothing more pain-relieving than a tape of whale song and a set of firmly gritted teeth? Men don't feel the need to pointlessly endure pain like that.

They don't say 'when I have that hernia operation, I'm going to refuse all drugs. I just want it to be as natural as possible'. Bollocks do they. They don't insist on 'experiencing' having their broken leg re-set. It bloody hurts.

Let me say now, for the record, there is nothing that wonderful about nature. It is red in tooth and claw, and, in this case, my face. It is well documented that everyone goes red in the face when they give birth, what they don't mention is the veins bulging out in your neck and the fact that you spurt quantities of shit all over the newly qualified Romanian midwife.

Don't forget bacteria and viruses are part of nature too, and no-one expects you to quietly endure the effects of smallpox whilst paying homage to the beauty and majesty of all-knowing 'nature'. Pus filled boils? Stick on a bit of whale song, have a hot bath. Piss off. Nature can be a bitch.

I gave birth to the first baby. The one thing that sticks in my mind from throughout that pregnancy is the fact that my skin was perfect. I looked fantastic. None of that 'throbbing areas of pain which give any social event you might attend an undercurrent of misery and insecurity' stuff, none of that at all. Mother hormone guarded me behind her tender aprons that year.

The actual birth wasn't fantastic. That fucking hurt. Sorry, did I mention that before? Believe me, it's worth repeating.
Then our son was here, pink and ugly as shit but I didn't realise that. I was just glad that the cast and crew of the time bandits had finally decided to stop filming a re-make at the back of my twat. It's like that, honestly. Lots of action, lots of stuff going on, but you can't see any of it. You feel it, though.
We moved in to our little house and played families.
I remember sitting in the living room on that first night, it was like an advert for a happy young family. We were surrounded by packing cases, telly on a box, cups of tea in big mugs, we had all that. But I felt miserable, I did. I felt wrong. I think it's because he was miserable, and I could sense it — fuck, I could probably SMELL it, what do you think, professor Winston? Here's a strange thing, it's just occurred to me, talking about smell. Alright, YOU weren't talking about smell, I was, but I'm calling the shots here. Tone didn't smell at all. Not at all. Not his feet, not his armpits, not any part of him. That sweaty man smell, that sexy musky man business that can swing the turn-on pendulum from fanny twitch to utter repugnance depending on whose musky man-ness you're smelling, that didn't exist with him. What the hell does that mean? No, I don't know either.
Somewhere during that first year of my first son's life, the acne came back. Everything was going wrong anyway, the acne was just the exclamation mark at the end of a long and sorry failure of a sentence. I came out from underneath the protective cover of those pregnancy hormones and discovered that my natural propensity to be a bit of a spotty bastard had kicked right back in.

Having been fading out for a few years, it came back with an added vengeance, as if to claim my face back from the clutches of my self-esteem. I was unhappy. I was in pain. I was living with a man who didn't smell of anything. Then I met Eva.

TRUST

She was six years younger than me, which makes her, at this particular period in time, eighteen. She was small and plump in a cute sort of way. Mousy hair, round cheeks, a certain plump-cheeked English rosy innocence about her, I'll give her that. She was no Marie Stopes for sure, but a pair of pert teenage tits more than makes up for not being one of the most influential women of the twentieth century. Well, it did for Tone, anyway.

She started off as a bit of a hanger-on. She didn't like being at her Dad's because of her step-Mum, and she didn't like being at her Mum's because of her step-Dad, so she hung out at our house. It was sort of fun at first, I made her laugh a lot, and she was company while I got through the long days of being a Mum. Shops, the park, tea, the shops, it's a long day being a Mum. Add to the mind-numbing fucking tedium the terrible soul-chewing guilt that you could even dream up the phrase 'mind-numbing fucking tedium' when thinking about your precious, wonderful children.

You love them, yes, you can love them and still find watching 'Fun Song Factory' forty-six times a day for a year and a half an appalling strain on your sanity and your soul.

Not being able to take a shit in peace for years on end corrodes your faculties.

You love them, yes, you love them, but Christ oh fucking

mighty, let me fucking sleep.
She kept me company through all of that.
She moved in eventually, sleeping on the sofa with her stuff in bin bags in the spare room. I liked it.
I liked not being alone.
I expect you can probably guess the way this is going, but I'll fill in the details.
The situation went on like that for months, Eva kept me company during the long days of the shopping centre and Tone kept me company at night. Well, he was there at least. He came home in the evening and took us to the beach at the weekends, but his mind was somewhere else. It's nice that image, isn't it, of the Dad fast asleep on the beach under his sun-hat? Is it shit. What it really means is 'my wife is currently chasing a toddler around a crowded beach, trying not to let him eat crustaceans and crap on the sunlounger while I fall asleep under my hat.'
Ditto Dad reading his newspaper.
I'm sorry, if you are a Dad, I'm not talking about ALL Dads here, just this one. Just Tone. And I'm sure, I'm positive, that the whole sunhat and newspaper thing when YOU do it, is a well-earned rest after giving your wife a lie-in and a cup of tea in bed this morning. Okay? Crumbs, you guys can be touchy. I'm talking about Tone here. He let me run about like that because his mind was somewhere else. I just didn't know where, not then.
I did love him, you know. If I hadn't, all this wouldn't matter. But I did.
He was blonde, with that reddish, coarse kind of body hair that goes with liver-coloured freckles on the back and forearms. Don't make crap 'ginger' jokes, that's not how it was. He had a body like autumn leaves. Heavily tattooed autumn leaves, maybe, but autumn leaves

nonetheless.

So I found out I was pregnant in the spring. All that coarse autumnal stuff must have really done the trick because I was having his blonde and freckly baby. Another baby, yes, there is one already.

There aren't any more, don't worry, I don't live in an enormous fucking shoe or something.

It was the year that everyone in the world fancied Natalie Umbruglia, the year she brought out 'Torn.' That song was everywhere. I sang it on Karaoke last Christrnas and I was shit, which pretty much sums up how that year went for me.

Eva came to my scan. She had become a better friend than her personality really allowed for, but I was new in town, I needed a friend. She was sweet to me.

I did like her you know. If I hadn't, all this wouldn't matter, but I did.

She came to my scan and listened to my fears, reassuring me and telling me how lucky I was. What a lovely family I had. The sort of family she'd never had but always wanted.

You can see where this is going, can't you?

I couldn't.

Now you're thinking: 'twat'.

Yes, a lot of people thought that too.

It started to dawn on me that Tone was having an affair. That would at least explain where his mind had been all these months. I told Eva, but she wouldn't believe it. How could he?

'You're so gorgeous,' she'd say, 'how could he ever want anyone else?'

Do you know what? In real life, they don't look meaningfully off camera while dramatic music plays.

There was no close-up on my face or smug but tell-tale smile playing menacingly around the edges of her mouth. Nothing like that, this was real life. I'm telling you, I just couldn't tell.

One day I found his camera under the bed, and it had a film in it. He had hidden it, that's the point, he didn't want me to see it. So I told Eva I was going to get it developed.

Back in the old days, for you thrusting eager young digital types, you had to take a camera to Boots the Chemists to get it developed before you could see what pictures you'd taken. You couldn't just scroll through them, deleting the ones where your Mum looks pissed off in the background. In those days, you had to keep them all.

I've got loads of pictures with my Mum looking pissed off in the background. I'd like to think it was just her face in repose, not contorted with a grimace for the capturing camera.

But I know my Mum.

Believe me, there's every chance that she was actually pissed off.

I told Eva I was going to get it developed. Secretly. I was going to find out what pictures he was taking that were so bloody secret they had to be kept under the bed.

'I'll come with you,' she said.

So we took it to Boots the chemist, I did the hour-long developing option, a touch more expensive but wow! To see all your photographs after only an hour? To anybody born before nineteen seventy-three, they can understand how that could be a novelty. Of course, there were polaroids, Where the photo comes out of a little slot in the bottom when you take it and appears like magic before your eyes. Yes, the bottom of the side board came out a bit wavy and orange and the red-eye is somewhat stark and unforgiving, but what fun! We didn't need quality in those days.

Me and Eva got the pictures developed. I opened the packet with her next to me, right there in the shop. I'd like to say I remember whether she looked apprehensive or whether she was sweating like a wilting English rose in a sauna, but honestly?

I can't remember.

This could be it, the moment of truth. The big bit. A big dramatic bit where something huge happens, some huge truth is known, I'm waiting for it. I'm willing it.

The pictures were of his Mum.

Never happens quite the way you want it to, does it?

Turns out he just put the camera under the bed to keep it out of the way.

Eva seems very happy on the walk home, something I didn't, at the time, attribute to relief.

HEY THERE, MICHAEL!

The acne came back.
This time, the pregnancy hormones are just having a wild hedonistic free-for-all, chucking out sickness and mood-swings and acne like empty coke cans from an eighteen-year-old's Ford Escort. This time, the acne in the mirror is contrasted with the English rose on the sofa. The mirror comes off worse. I feel like shit.
There comes a point, for all acne sufferers, when you have simply been there too many times before. Each spot, each point of your face, each tiny movement in the tectonic plates that make up the Earth's crust of your shitty appearance, you have been there before.
Take the ones that come up on your top lip, the ones that make your eyes water.
The ones that come up down the sides of your chin, making you look like a glue sniffer.
The ones that, in some unpleasantly symetrical symbiosis, manage to appear simultaneously on matching but opposite sides of your face. Like both of your eyebrows. As if God couldn't be bothered and just did one side, and then folded your face in half to make it print like one of those pictures you did when you were a kid.
Then the cat got fleas. Me and Tone had a cat, a ginger

thing, did I tell you? It got fleas about this time. Cat fleas are bastards. Cats generally are not good news in my opinion. People will tell you, 'Oh, they just look after themselves.' That's true enough, but it does result in leaving out food and scraping up shit and coping with fleas for an animal which does not seem to exist. Their shit smells terrible as well. That's probably why they're the pet of choice for the over-seventies, it's the only smell in the world which can mask that tell-tale old-lady aroma.

So, the fleas. I get bitten by fleas. Fleas love me. Every summer since I was eight years old I have spent the first three weeks finding slowly swelling red lumps on my ankle bone and forearms, as the summer bugs wake up. This summer, it was the fleas.

While Eva was lounging about in her pleasingly plump youthful loveliness, I was struggling with a corrugated face and swelling red legs. It was a whole body pebble-dash. If a working class person had made a lot of money and decorated me, I couldn't look worse. I might as well have glued ducks of gradually increasing size down the side of my buttocks, so unappetising was my exterior décor.

I know I should have gone to the doctor, but do you know what? I didn't want anyone to look at it. Imagine that. Having something you're so desperate to hide, something you never, ever want another human soul to gaze upon, something which causes you shame and misery beyond Gary Glitter's most shameful and miserable dreams, having that something GLUED TO YOUR FUCKING FACE. It hurts.

The thought of a doctor peering at my shame, touching it, acknowledging it, even having to go out of the house

without make-up on, Christ, I couldn't bear it. Coupled with that the knowledge that you're JUST BEING SILLY, that hurts. The knowledge that IT'S ONLY A FEW SPOTS, that you're not only ugly but a neurotic twat with a shallow obsessive nature as well.
I hated myself that summer.
I told Eva all about it, of course, and she reassured me.
'They don't show,' she'd say.
'Don't squeeze them, you'll make them worse.'
We would sit up late at night, watching films, and I would make her laugh. I could make her laugh and laugh and laugh. We had a friend called Gemma — yeah, that Gemma, and we would do the sort of stuff that I don't usually do, make small talk, crap talk, it felt shallow but it was human contact. Even that bloke on the solitary round-the-world yacht race cried when his bloody cat died.
I was lonely, okay? I liked the company.
Fuck, let's cut to the chase.
This story's not even about them anyway.
Yeah, they were having an affair, bollocks to them both, the bastards.
They left, and there I was. Pregnant, alone, frightened, pebble-dashed.
Why did I start writing about those two anyway? Oh, the Gemma thing. I hate my housemate. The one I'm currently watching a documentary with, in a silence which is not so much in deference to the stimulating nature of the television, and more the result of a personality vacuum. I'll get back to this bit in a minute.
I wasn't pregnant for very long after that, because a few months later Michael was born. I tell you, if you've ever been in a situation where you've felt a bit disappointed

that you didn't have a partner, Valentine's days maybe, or standing in front of a waterfall at sunset, try having a baby with no-one but a surly midwife, who can't wait to go off shift because its four in the morning, for company. No really, try it, I implore you.

I hadn't been to the doctors or done anything official about my pregnancy, so when I turned up at the hospital there was no record of a pregnant woman with my name. I thought they'd say 'never mind dear, come in, you look in pain' and lead me tenderly to a bed. Did they bollocks. What they actually did was run about panicking that there was no record of me anywhere, I thought they were going to send me home at this point on the grounds that I did not exist. It was like that scene from 'airplane' where they all assume 'crash positions'. I thought a midwife with her tits out was going to rush hysterically across my field of vision.

Eventually they took my physical presence as evidence of my genuine existence and allowed me to lie down on a bed. They left me there for a long time. I remember lying on the bed in agony, feeling more alone than any waterfall at sunset could ever make me feel, and hearing the screams of the woman giving birth in the room next door. They left me there.

When I was squeezing him out, they managed to turn up. One woman took the epidural away and the pain hit me like, well, like your body squeezing a human being out of a tiny hole. Don't read this if you ever want to have a baby, don't read this next sentence. Just skip to the next paragraph, go on.

It feels like Geoff Capes sticking his hand up your arse and ripping out one of your internal organs.

Mirriam Stoppard won't tell you that, but it does.

This woman took my drugs away, and I knew what was coming, and fuck, I begged. I begged like the last coward on a bayonet, let me tell you, every human has a point when they'll beg.
'It'll take longer if I leave it there,' she said icily.
'FUUUUCK YEEEEEW!' I replied, admittedly not helping our frosty relationship.
'We'll be here for hours,' she said. I'm not lying. If you're a midwife I'm sure, I'm positive, that when YOU'RE on shift at four in the morning confronted by a single Mum, you're as kind and as compassionate as anyone could ever wish. I'm not talking about all midwives. Just this one. Crumbs, you guys can be touchy.
She took away the drugs and my body was ripped apart by Edwina Currie driving a steam train wildly out of control through my lower body. There was a slither like a giant tadpole slopping out between my thighs, and suddenly the inside of my body felt very cold. Like when you're sitting next to someone and they move away, that sort of cold. Another human body is suddenly not touching you any more. Then Michael was there.
Michael was there, and nothing else mattered.
I was in love.

I called him Michael for a reason. There's this song by Kate Bush, its called 'Moments of Pleasure'. Me and Tone used to listen to that a lot, it says stuff that everyone can identify with, but when you do, it feels like its talking just to you. 'We sat up all night talking about it' was one line. Yeah, we did that.
'Hey there Michael, do you really love me?' was another.
You see where I'm going with this now, don't you?
It's crap, its a cliché, but its that resonance thing again,

isn't it?

That song we listened to, all that stuff we did, everything we had, that must have meant something.

It must have meant something, because its here, its alive, and I mean REALLY alive —— its a person. Its resonating so much I won't get a decent night's sleep for six months. That's resonance, baby. It didn't just float up into the ether, all that flotsam of the past, it meant something. Sometimes, those ripples, you can hardly feel them, but they're still there.

He still doesn't know. Don't tell him.

HOUSEMATE

I had to get a housemate to help pay the bills after that, so I asked some friends. I didn't want anyone who was still friends with Eva, I didn't want anyone bringing her smell into the house, so I asked some people who had taken my side in the whole sorry business.
Guess who moved in?
Of course it was, old dry toast herself. This mistress of bland. The person who proves that the words 'human interest' aren't necessarily compatible.
We're still here, we're still watching the documentary, we're back from the past now and that little bit about the background is finished. It was a bit of a chore, to be honest, maybe I shouldn't have done it. But it's done now, and you probably feel as if you know me a little better. So no harm done.
The point is, why is Gemma involved in all of this? I'll tell you.
I've started to suspect she isn't as loyal a friend as the dry-toast-eating twat makes out. I'm starting to suspect that my house isn't washed entirely clean of lies and betrayal, and the smell of dishonesty smells like a dirty housemate's feet. Shit.
She's lying to me.
I think Eva may still have a window into my life, a life she tore apart but still wants to peer at, and I think Gemma is that window, I think she's relaying information about me

back to Eva. Is that paranoid? All the evidence I have is a few words, a look, a shoulder squeeze. Judge Judy would fucking piss on me, I know it. I'm not even sure how reasonable it is for me to care this much, but I do. I do care. It eats away at me, just to think that the fungus of betrayal is still creeping up my walls,
fed by Gemma on some sort of moisture that certainly didn't come off her toast.
She's done a few weird things. She hides sometimes when she makes phone calls. She squeezes her boyfriend's shoulder if he says something suspicious. Which is more suspicious, in my opinion.
'I saw Eva in that phone box by the cinema, that's where their flat is,' she says, out of the blue. Thank you for reminding me about the collapse of love and hope and trust in my desperate life, I was watching a documentary here.
'Sally told me. Their flat's by the cinema. Apparently its really nice.'
Good, good. I'm glad. I'm lonely and suffering from depression brought on by chronic fatigue and you're telling me about an arsehole's living conditions. Go for it, tact lady.
'By the cinema? Christ, I don't want to bump into them. I'd be forced to rip her face off and ram it up her fat backside.'
Gemma laughs, but nervously. I think she knows I'm only half-joking. She's bitten off more than she can chew with this, I think, she's out of her depth. Maybe she likes playing it close to the edge, I get that feeling sometimes. She likes being close enough to the storm to hear the windows rattle.
'Eva's besotted.'

Right, this is as much as I can take. Besotted she may be, but I was pregnant, and surely that should take precedence? Unfortunately, a besotted eighteen year old with big tits may be somewhat more alluring than a pebble-dashed pregnant chronic piss-taker. Which I am. 'Don't tell me that, it makes me feel sad.' There, there you are housie, have the truth and see if it makes a dent in your elephant hide. Pick up on it, Gemma, you're winding me up.
'Sally told me.'
Yeah right.
'Did that tall man phone?' she is smirking now, she's bloody smirking. I'm just too English to chuck her out, the English can't chuck people out until they're absolutely sure. Hitler, we were sure about, yes, he was a fucker. But we have to be sure. Christ, what if we OFFEND somebody? 'No, he didn't phone back. I knew he wouldn't.' No wonder she can eat dry toast, her throat is lubricated by the moist bile of her own repugnance.
'He might.'
Her voice is high-pitched now, she's got something on me, I know it. Has she spoken to Phil? Has her brother indicated a desire to move to Kurdistan to avoid the knowledge that a spotty woman in a small Sussex town is constantly being asked by every aquaintance if he has FUCKING PHONED. He hasn't. For the record, he hasn't.
'Sally told me something else as well.'
She's still friends with Eva, isn't she? I know, I know, I can't chuck her out, I can't. What if I'm wrong?
I bet she is though.
Which means Eva knows stuff about me, stuff she has no right to know.
Like the fact I cry and cry and cry and I can't get over it

and I miss him I miss him I miss him. Stuff that only your housemate knows.

The sort of stuff you don't want the twat who stole your life knowing.

Am I going over the top? This is the relationship equivalent of the bloody Somme, even my metaphors are war-related.

Anyway, the documentary, my house, a year after all that Tone and Eva crap.

Huge boil, tanned, smelly, lying housemate. Here we go.

Fleas are still jumping.

Boil still throbbing.

Then the bombshell…

LUCKY

'Tone and Eva have won the lottery. They're going to Mexico.'
........pardon?

'They've won a couple of thousand. I dunno how much exactly, but they've got a new jeep.'
How the FUCK does she know that?
'Sally told me.'
Oh, right. Yeah RIGHT.
How the FUCK does she know that?
Come on, Professor Winston, sniff test please. Human smell is vastly underrated but I can't smell anything except flea-powder. How does she always know all this stuff?
All that Britishness, that inability to explode, that leaves me at this precise point. Gemma didn't expect this, I don't think, she was just looking for another good opportunity to smirk at the emotionally shattered freak show. But I still can't explode at her, I mean, what if I'm WRONG?
So I just start to scream, strangely enough not waking my two tiny children asleep upstairs.
Words tumble over words in an incoherent jumble, I'm screaming, tugging at my hair, pulling out clumps of it and stamping my feet.
You really do all those things when true anger hits you, it sounds crap, it sounds like a cliché, yeah yeah, you pulled

out your hair and stamped your feet, but I did. If I hadn't, all this wouldn't matter,
but I did.
This anger hurts, it hurts like someone with a painful boil just pulled out a clump of their own hair. I
How dare they win the lottery? When it happened, when it all came out that they'd been betraying me for months and months in my own house, when that all came out, everyone said, 'Oh, they'll get their comeuppance.'
Yeah, RIGHT.
This isn't chance, to me.
This is life saying 'you're clearly a cunt', and dealing me a hand appropriate to my status as an undeserving arsehole. All that struggle, all that loneliness, all that whole year of being alone with the children, with a NEW BORN BABY for Christ's bloody sake, and this is what happens.
The tall man doesn't phone, and those two get everything they ever dreamed of, plus the ability to sleep longer than an hour a night without having to make squash for a screaming red-faced midget. Bastards, fucking fucking bastards.
Gemma looks a bit alarmed by the screaming and the sobbing and the hair-pulling, but she hasn't moved. She just sits in the swivel chair, stunned into immobility and staring at me like a hedgehog on the M4. Any minute now, and she'll roll up into a ball and I will just juggernaught over her head. She looks scared.
I phone Tone's Mum. She's sweet, she tells me not to cry, but the tears won't stop tonight.
'I wish I could 'elp you,' says Tone's Mum. It's upsetting her, I can tell, but I don't care about anything right now except the large piece of hot lead expanding in my

diaphragm. Maybe I'm really going mad this time, I feel it. I can't breathe, I can't think straight.

Those people, those people who stole everything you ever had, they've just got a little bit more.

I resign, I do, I fucking resign from the human race.

Gemma stares at me, centre parting pointing at me as if to say, 'Who's THAT mad fucking bastard?' Even her hair is lifeless. I have strands of my own hair, short and black at the root like my crappy life, clinging to my hands because they've been sweating. Strands of hair stick to the tears on my cheeks, and whisper down to rest on my arms. I look like Oliver Reed in a bad sixties werewolf movie.

But I am actually genuinely frightening, because I'm real. I'll tell you what I did, I hate to remember it, but I'll tell you for the sake of that whole 'at least I'm not the only one' thing. Maybe you've done it too, and you'll know.

My legs stand up and start walking. I'm not exaggerating, they do it on their own. They take me to the kitchen cupboard, and my arms go up, I watch them go up, and my hands open the cupboard. My hands go in and find what they are looking for; my sleeping pills.

'Oh my God,' I think, 'I'm going to commit suicide.'

All this loneliness, all year, I've wanted to do it, but I haven't. I wanted to stay for the boys, I didn't want them to be left with a lying father and an evil stepmother. But this, this is too much. Life is too unfair, I can't live if this is what life is, I'm sorry.

'Crikey,' I think, 'I'm really doing it. This is unexpected, I've got to be up in the morning'.

My hands open the little jar, and I see what is inside.

It's empty.

Thank God, now my body will have to behave itself.

But I still have the burning, unbearable agony of fury and

misery to deal with so I put on a video. Always put on a video, its amazing what it can do. When you need any reality other than your own, its there. Never fails you. How on earth did they cope before they had videos?
Books, I suppose.
Anyway.
I put on 'Jaws.' I concentrate on not thinking, not looking at Gemma.
Gemma gets up very carefully when she realises I have started to calm down, on the outside at least. She asks the question, we'd all ask it, but its so crap, so obviously wrong.
'You OKAY?'
'Yeah. I'm going to watch Jaws and not think about it,' I tell her.
She squashes her bottom lip against her teeth for a minute, looking awkward and almost sorry for me. I nearly regret letting her see me like that, she's bitten off more than she can chew. Then she goes to bed.
This is the saddest I've ever been, I think. Sadder than when it first happened, because at least then there was a chance that in the future it would get better. Well, we're in the future now and its not better at all. In fact, it's bloody worse. So that's enough looking forwards to the future for me, if it turns out to be this shit. This is what I was waiting for, life, you piss-taking bastard.
Somebody said once that depression is anger without the energy. They were right.
You're still angry, still churning up your guts with it, but you're too tired to scream about it anymore. It's a tired-out anger. An old tiger in the zoo. Once it could have bitten a man's head clean off, but now it just sort of mopes about and gets fat.

I watch Jaws.

That night in Wales, that other sad night in another stupid story, I watched Woody Allen videos for eight hours. The night Tone left, I watched Jennifer Saunders. Any story other than my own.

This is a good bit, the bit on the boat where they're comparing battle scars, I like that bit. Roy Schnieder pulls up his jumper and all he's got is an appendix scar, it's too crap, it's not good enough. The other two, they're getting on great with their huge shark bites and stuff. Roy is crap, and he knows it. Fuck, animals don't even want to bite him.

I love the look on his face when he pulls his jumper back down. He's not jealous exactly, he just feels a bit silly. A bit not good enough.

This is a good bit too, Robert Shaw spewing up his guts and screaming like a girl, that scared me when I was a kid. The toughest bloke on screen gets it, and that's pretty scary because if he can get it, anything could happen.

Then it happens.

This is where my life changes, right here, at this single moment. I don't think many people can pin point that exact second in their lives, can say 'this moment, here, this is where it changed' but I can. This is the moment when I started wanting to be alive.

I've wondered since whether the fact I was watching that bit in Jaws was like that thing you learn about on English literature courses, where the back ground to the action echoes the actual action itself. Big thunderstorms during an argument, that sort of stuff. You know. Prophetic fallacy. Or is it pathetic fallacy? Prophetic would make more sense, like it's predicting the future. Pathetic, what's that? Latin for feelings, from 'pathos' I think. The feeling

fallacy? And why fallacy? This is fucking true. I think our tutor was just having a laugh with us, 'tell 'em any old crap and they'll lap it up!' he'd chortle in the staff room. Then we'd scribble out our three thousand words in cheap biro while the Freshers cried over rugby players in the room next door. Anyway, it really, really was that big dramatic moment in Jaws, I could make up something else, something more appropriate to my own storyline, but I won't. It was that precise moment, and I know that because I remember exactly what happened next.
The phone rings. Everything changes, here, with this ring.
Can you hear it?
Ring ring. Ring ring. Ring ring.
This is my life saying, 'Okay, you've had enough of this shit. Have a ring ring, it'll do you good.'
Ring ring. I pick it up.
'......hello?'
I never answer the telephone by saying my telephone number, my Mum does that. Despite all the other ways in which I'm like my Mum, I never answer the phone like her. I have to have some small sense of identity, for Christ's sake. I never organise my saucepans in size order, either. Yeah, yeah, it'd stop them falling over in the cupboard, but I'm my own person, a different person to my Mum, and that proves it. Being pissed off a lot? Well, yes, in some ways we are peas in a bloody pod. 'Hello. I want to come and see you. Are you busy? Can I come round now?'
It's the tall man. He's on the phone, right now.
'Erm, well, it's late. I can't stay up too late because of the kids. I get up early.'
What am I SAYING?

'I know, but I suddenly had to see you. I think we need to have a conversation.'

He's like that, I know that from the small amount I DO know. He's either silent or having a conversation, there's no middle ground, no tossing out the odd remark.

'That sounds nice. Late night conversations are usually the most interesting.'

Do I hit the right note? A bit flirty, not too much, slightly reserved? Intriguing? Not a bit of it, my heart is so often on my sleeve I use Velcro. Put your heart away, woman. Play the mysterious card. 'I'll leave now, I can be at yours in twenty minutes.'

'Okay, I'll just watch the end of Jaws.'

'Jaws?'

'I was watching Jaws. But I'd rather have a conversation.'

I hear him expell a breath through his nose, not a laugh so much as a small acknowledgement.

'Okay, see you in a bit.'

'See you.'

I keep the phone by my ear until it goes hum, then put it down slowly.

I've got twenty minutes to get it together. I go to the kitchen. I have a mirror leant up against the kitchen window, a big thing in the shape of a fish Tone's sister made us for the bathroom. It's got a sort of lumpy greenish-blue frame with the texture of papier mache, she made it for the bathroom but ironically water has made the bottom of the frame disintegrate. Still, it's a big mirror, and I put my make-up on downstairs because I need to be where the kids are. Casually going upstairs on your own for ten minutes at a stretch is a luxury traditionally only afforded to those who are not single parents to two toddlers.

I have to stretch over the sink to look in the mirror, so to my mind I am constantly slightly red in the face and strained looking, with raised eyebrows and plumbing wedged in my collar-bone. I know I
don't look like that all the time, but the image persists.
The boil is pretty angry. Tear tracks are still visible in my blusher, and my hair is thinner than it was.
Luckily I have two plus points to work with; my hair is thick and coarse anyway, cut roughly into a short sort of style that looks good messed up a bit. I cut it myself, I hate that prim and tidy thing hairdressers do to you. Tidy hair, that doesn't say sexy to me. These days all the girls straighten their hair, God knows why, they look like a whole generation of librarians.
My other plus point is my face. The face under the acne, I mean. My great-grandfather had an enormous jaw bone and jutting cheekbones that made him look like a comic book super hero. My Dad got that too, from his Dad, and they both passed it on to me. It doesn't work quite as well on a woman, my face is straight lines, no Marilyn-feminine baby-soft curves for me — but it's a good face. Structured like a well-built log cabin, built to last. White teeth, big smile, Roman nose, I can carry a few boils with pride. Let me tell you, my friends, I've had to.
I spend ten minutes putting make-up on, and Phil is right. There's a texture to it, it hurts like hell, but I can still look good. Stick a comic-relief red nose on a log cabin, it still looks pretty noble.
I am trembling with happiness. Adrenalin clouds my brain and blots out all other thought, which is a nice diversion for a single Mum with a boil problem. My hands are shaking with excitement which actually makes me look nicer.

Can I give you a beauty tip? This isn't some crap woman's magazine, but let me tell you something that all those adverts trying to separate you from your money don't tell you. There's one thing that no amount of cream or powder can really duplicate; adrenalin-charged joy. And THAT my friends is the ultimate in sexy. You want your eyes to sparkle and your skin to glow? Don't waste your money, girls. There's a quicker way.
Have a wank.
There's no time for wanking now, I'm charged up with adrenalin anyway, I don't need to.
I leave the face in the mirror, and sit in my swivel chair. It's a good chair to receive visitors in, both
loungy and commanding, swivelly and focal-pointing, it's a good chair.
I sit in it and lounge a bit. Think sexy, a bit of posing is sexy. My brother's a computer programmer, he would never pose in his life. He's cool, my brother, he's funny in a dry kind of way, but he's not sexy. Despite the jaw and stuff, Christ, my whole family have that jaw. Even my nan and my Mum who simply married into the family and weren't related to the super-hero at all.
The back door bangs, fuck, he's come in the back door. He's been here before with Phil, she always comes in through the back door. I don't swivel round, I can hear Mel Gibson in my head, you know that bit in 'Braveheart' when they're waiting for the English to approach and they know they're okay because they've got those massive spear things. 'Hold....hold....' says Mel in a Scottish accent in my head. He's always there when I don't want to rush into something. 'Hold....hold...'
Here he is, the tall man. He collapses on the floor by my feet, out of breath and panting.

He puts a hand on my knee. No, honestly, he does. If he hadn't, all this story would be pointless. I mean, why make it up? But he really did.
'I HAD to see you, I can't get you out of my head. I can't stop thinking about you.'
Half an hour ago, this was the saddest day of my life.
'Please tell me what to do. I want to just jump on you, but I don't know how.'
There's been no love in my life for over a year.
No sex for even longer. Half an hour ago I tried to kill myself, would you be here if you knew that? I'm a different person now. All that rubble of the past, I've kind of wall-papered over that for now, so I smile and do the light-hearted-and-witty thing I do so well, the thing that, I know from his sister, made him fancy me in the first place. That and the jaw-bone I can only assume. He must like super- heroes or something. Whatever, its all good news for me.
'I can't tell you what to do, Danny. If you want to ask me out, ask me. I can't tell you to.'
'I just wanted to discuss it with you first.'
I know I've got him, he wouldn't be here otherwise. So I play a little bit, savouring the moment. 'I'm not discussing it. If you want me to beg you to ask me out, the door is over there.'
This is playing it close to the edge, but it's fun. I'm charged up with it all, fuck, this is fun.
'What should I do?'
'You should have thought about that before you came over.'
He looks at me beseechingly and reminds me fleetingly of my parents' dog. What do his eyes tell me? Is he driven by millennia of instinct, acting on impulses that his body

can interpret better than his mind? Life, death, mating, evolution, what brought him to my door?
On second thoughts, maybe he just needs a shit.
He looks up at me with those wolvine eyes. Wolfish in beauty, not in temperament.
'I want to just.....just kiss you.'

I'm out of my swivel chair like Jack Robinson, whoever he was, but apparently he was fast.
We fall into each other's arms and on to the waiting floor. Even the carpet feels pleased.

We're not actually on the carpet. Phil, in her honesty and her wisdom, decided that even though I wasn't having sex with anybody it was probably prudent to have somewhere comfortable to do it, should the opportunity present itself. I have the housemate in one bedroom, the queen of beige, presider over all that is mediocre, eater of tasteless toast. In the other bedroom, in my one double bed, sleep my two children and I. This isn't a sob story, it's the arrangement that we have. I've cobbled this shit together out of the shattered rubble of my life, and I'm proud of it. So Phil gave me a chair-bed, a chair that turns into a bed. It's a squat, ugly, brown squishy sort of affair, like a tribal elder on a documentary about Peru. It looks like its seen a bit of life, supported a few arses and will last a damn sight longer than any of the other furniture. It's here, in the living-room, pulled out as far as it will go and Danny's feet are still pressing pause on the video on the other side of the room.
Fuck, he's tall.
I can't remember pulling out the chair-bed, but we must have done because we're in it now. When you feel like this,

even brown corduroy can't spoil it.

There's a book my Mum used to like called 'Precious Bane,' about a girl with a hare lip. I used to like skipping to the very last paragraph, where she gets her man despite looking like shit. I liked that bit, and I'm liking this.
He is my Kester Woodseaves the weaver, and he kisses me full upon the mouth. His eyes look comical this close up, like a cartoon chipmunk or something. He did kiss me on the mouth, except it didn't end there. We had sex.
I'm sure Kester Woodseaves and that girl with the hare lip from 'Precious Bane' did too, but this being a modern novel, I'm actually going to describe it to you. Sign of the times, eh?
He's got a long face, Danny. A friendly hang-dog kind of face. He's always got that look of canine apology like he's just done a crap on the carpet or something. His eyes are big brown liquified conkers, set in an Alsatian face.
He is wolfish, with his black chest hair and long spine, but not the big bad kind, not that. The real big bad wolf in my life was yellow and sturdy like a healthy labrador puppy. Yellow like the sun is yellow, beautiful and blinding. Ironic, eh? Things never turn out the way you expect.
But this man is all things dark. Not like bad things are dark, just like the night is dark, just like some things are dark just because they are. His mouth is the thing that I can't stop looking at sometimes, sometimes in that half-light of late-night falling in love, that orange light, he looks so beautiful to me. His teeth are perfect and white, his lips are full without being bloated — think Marilyn Monroe rather than Bella Emberg. He has that thing when he smiles like Elvis had, like Will Smith has, that little pucker under each cheek bone. Its a great trick if you've

been born with it. It's simultaneously schoolboyish and sensual, like a naughty ten-year-old who looks a bit like a boy you remember fancying at school.

No, that's not right, that sounds a bit pervy. You know what I mean. When grown men have that vulnerable look to them, it only works if they're otherwise pretty sorted — too much vulnerable can be bad. You don't want a sap on your hands, you just want the opportunity to mop them up occasionally.

Danny was like that.

He looked thinnish with his clothes on, but now I can see that's not the case. He's tall, Danny, he's a walking talking optical illusion. Having sex with him is like looking hard at one of those pictures of a vase that's also a face....he's thin...but his legs are muscular....he's thin.....hang on, I can see a broad chest there......there's a beauty to those first moments of discovery. I can understand why some people get addicted to them.

As long as his face doesn't start to actually turn into a vase, that'd scare the crap out of me.

We are on the floor, and he is squashing the breath out of me. Really tall men, they look great, but they squash the breath out of you. It's all really sexy and stuff like that, he smells good, he feels warm and slightly sweaty on the middle of his back the way men do, but even now my boil is intruding on my thoughts. He's kissing me hard, which I'm sure has worked in the past on women who don't have a small nugget of painful poison under the skin of their bottom lip, but I do.

I'm also starting to grow concerned about the state of the face as a whole.

The tip of his nose, whilst being generally as attractive and desirable as the rest of his body, has lost good favour

with me due to having wiped the cover-up from a spot on my cheek. He keeps trying to do that thing, that sexy romantic thing where the man cups the woman's face with his hand. Nice, nice in films where the girls tend not to have smeared rice pudding over their cheeks before filming. I am conscious of his thumbs on my cheekbone, the bone is the most painful part of the face to have a spot. I believe the same is true of having a tattoo but to be honest I've never had one. I can't think of a tattoo I'd like to have. Definitely not one of those elongated triangle celtic ones, the ones twenty-somethings have on their backs, across the top of their jeans. Not actually on the jeans, you know what I mean, on the skin, but hoping their jeans will slip down and their racy but also symbolic and meaningful body art will be revealed to an adoring public. Unfortunately, they've all got one too.
I don't want his thumb to encounter bumpy where it should only be smooth.
I don't want him to think 'what the fuck's all this lumpy shit on her face?'
I don't want, most of all, to be thinking these thoughts in the middle of kissing the man of my dreams.
I wish he would just start touching me up, anything to make him leave my face alone.
Thank fuck, he's going for the tits. Not that they're anything to write home about, but at least they're spot-free. Now I need an excuse to get up and quickly check the face. I don't want him to pull away, gaze tenderly into my eyes, reach to pull a strand of my hair from my cheek, and vomit.
'I just need to — to — do a wee' I say in desperation. Well, what do you want me to say? 'Let me just make sure your nose hasn't rubbed concealer stick off the more

unpleasantly concave blemishes which tarnish every facet of my existence, back in a mo'? I know that even in this moment of urgency, my compulsion to squeeze will let me down. 'Just squeeze the fucking thing, just fucking do it.' Christ, I'm not going back down there oozing moisture down one check and smiling through the pain. Leave me alone, you pocky bastards.

The bathroom mirror re-assures me by having the foresight to be utterly filthy. I can't see much, but I can see that good father adrenalin has blessed me and the eyes are outshining the acne tonight. I flush the toilet for the sake of authenticity and go back into his arms. I resolve to lose myself in the moment, not to dwell on my skin or things which might distract from the excitement of one's dreams actually coming true, which must be a rare enough occurrence to merit at least a little bit of losing. Forget about the spots, you stupid cow. Nothing can spoil this, our precious first night of what could be love.

I pull away suddenly.

'Christ, I've just thought. You're not allergic to flea bites are you?'

I don't want to you to think I've got it in for insects, particularly. In fact, insects have played an unusually large part in my life, and I don't think I have been the poorer for it. We had frogs, when I was a kid. Big bloody frogs, and we fed them on locusts and crickets. My Dad loves all animals, all living things, really — nature, plants, if it's alive then he'll be all for it, believe me.

We got the frogs from the local pet shop. This was the seventies, remember, a time when they still sold puppies in pet shops, smoked fags in hospital and had real monkeys on Clacton peer. During the seventies, we had exotic pets, everywhere was covered in huge ashtrays and

I had my photo taken with a tiny skinny monkey on a string on summer holiday. Don't judge us, things were different back then. I recently took my children to the zoo and a sign on a red-eared terrapin cage described how, thirty years ago, people would buy them from pet shops with no idea how to look after them and they would die.

My Mum and Dad bought two from our pet shop in nineteen-seventy five and fed them raw mince. They died. The big frogs died too, but we did spend one fantastic year watching the one that survived stalking his locusts and then digesting them slowly while the back bit still wriggled. That was what we did for entertainment in those days, we only had a portable telly.

So for one year our bathroom was full of crickets and locusts at night. Dad put them in the bathroom because of the noise they made, all that humming and singing and squeaking all night. Christ only knows how the Greeks get any sleep at all. I don't remember my Mum minding, which is weird, because my Mum minds if she needs a piss and you happen to be in the bathroom. Fill it with screaming smelly insects, however, and she won't say a word. She's like that my Mum. She only sweats the small stuff.

A fascination with ants looms large in my memories of that time. This was fuelled partly by a story my Mum told us about when she was a child in Africa. Occasionally, my Mum would break off from playing 'Chucky Egg' or whatever beeping game she was currently obsessed with, to tell a fantastical tale of life overseas. Then she'd pick up her dropped Rothmans, dust the fag ash off her flesh-coloured tights and go back to her incessant clacking. She's got long finger-nails my Mum, a lot of her gaming activities involve clacking. Breaking off occasionally to

say:
'Peter, the bloody dog needs a shit again.'
My parent's marriage has been peppered with dogs that always need to shit.
Mum had a long-running dispute with the woman upstairs, throughout my whole childhood it seemed, over whether the shit in the garden of the flats was dog shit or fox shit. Esme from number eight was putting her money firmly on dog shit, Mum's dog in particular. Mum, as I recall, erred more on the side of fox-shit, which moved her on more than one occasion to refer to our neighbour as a 'fucking old bag with fat legs'. To be fair to Mum, I have many memories of her engaged in coping with and disposing of dog shit, so perhaps it was the foxes. Who knows?
Back to the fantastical story. Apparently, these enormous red African ants were goose-stepping around the toilet while she was sitting on it, and she had to scream for her Dad. Her Dad rescued her in an enormous pair of ant-proof boots, and to this day she can't abide the sight of a man with bare feet. Red ants are one of those childhood fear-stories, aren't they? Along with poison ivy. Red ants and poison ivy, nasty business. Don't touch them! Motorways? Go for your life. Take a picnic.
She was like the opposite of Uncle Albert in Only Fools and Horses, my Mum. We WANTED her to tell her fantastical tales, but she never seemed to want to. Not very often, anyway. I think she was too busy getting the washing-up done and the beds made to remember she'd once been a person. For a person who has lived such a strange and complex life and experienced the wonder of so many diverse cultures and languages, she's spent a disproportionate amount of her adult life clacking her

brains out on Chucky Egg.

So, fleas. Bloody fleas.

I definitely prefer ants to fleas. We had ants every summer when I was a kid and I grew quite attached to them. I would put a sweet on the floor overnight and marvel at how it would be black with ants in the morning. Poke it, and all the ants would run away revealing your sweet like a tiny sunrise.

Like I said, we only had a portable telly.

How do they find stuff like that? Stuff that, relatively to them, is miles away? My husband couldn't even find Truro on holiday last year, we had to drive back to the wind turbines and start again. There was one story about ants which particularly fascinated me — bear with me, we'll get back to the sex bit in a minute, don't worry. This ant trick never worked for me, if you've ever managed it successfully, there's no need to contact me, my life is fuller now.

My teacher told me, when I was nine, that if you draw a circle using chalk around a single ant, it won't be able to escape. It will be trapped in the circle, running round and round, but if you wait long enough something wonderful will happen. All the other ants, it's hill-mates I suppose, will come and rescue it, finding it like a dropped sweet under a nine-year-old's bed. They will build a living bridge out of their own connected bodies until they reach their imprisoned comrade and pull him out. Fleas don't do that, fleas are crap. Yeah, yeah, they can jump higher than a house, relatively. So what? We can build a fucking house. I don't see fleas building anything.

So I tried this, hundreds of bloody times. The paving stones outside our flat were covered in tiny chalk circles, but the bastards always managed to scramble out. Who says they can't climb over, chalk? They can climb up the side of a building, for God's sake. Chalk is child's play to them, its a warm-up. But that didn't stop me trying. I kind of liked to see them panicking, running about furiously looking for an escape route. The old airplane 'crash positions' panic again, and an ant with its tits out flashes across your field of vision. I used to feel sad whenever I killed an ant, and imagine mummy ant and baby ant waiting anxiously at home for daddy ant who never returns. Now I know that ant society is more of a super-structure, with all the workers just slogging it out for one big momma and no individuality amongst them. More like cells in one brain. I feel relieved now I have this information, now I know this, nothing could ever be as bad as it seems.

That same teacher who told me that wrote a quote from Shakespeare in my little leaver's book when I left primary school. I didn't understand it at the time, but it resonates with me now. If it didn't, all this wouldn't matter. But it does.

'This above all: to thine own self be true,' he wrote.

'Oh,' I thought. 'Great.'

Truth can be painful, but it's good fresh air to the skin under the plaster, so rip off that facade and be done with it. Remember that bloke? That crap writer I told you about at the beginning? It worked for him. Sometimes time just unravels it all out for you like a loom-made rug. Here it is! That was the point of that bit! Thank you, fate, I understand it a tiny bit better now. So no more adventure spy stories, let's communicate a fragment of truth here.

Okay, back to the sex part. You've been very patient. Unless you've just skipped straight to this bit, in which case there are going to be some things later on that don't make much sense to you. Fine, if you can live with that, just carry on. I admit I listen to albums like that, a song here, a song there, sometimes one song over and over again.

'They've put a lot of thought into which songs go after each other,' my friend Steve would berate me. 'You're supposed to listen to it all the way through, see how it all goes together.' Nah, bollocks to that. I'll just put on 'Fast Car' sixty-eight times in a row, if you don't mind. He does mind.

I'm back in his arms, aren't I? The wolf-eyed man, I mean, not my mate Steve. I did get off with him once at college, but to be honest I got off with most people at college, and I can't write about them all. Wolf man then.

I admit I'm not quite sure how to write about all this, I mean, it's a bit private, isn't it? Try writing in detail about YOUR sex life for a load of virtual strangers sometime, go on, try it. It's a nightmare. Okay, so you haven't pretended you were going to and then bottled it at the last post, maybe you're not to be blamed for feeling a little cheated. Do you really need to know the details before you feel satisfied? My Mum's going to read this, you know. Spare her feelings, I beg you.

We had sex. Right there, on the living-room floor. Don't worry, the kids were upstairs asleep, they didn't see a thing. I'll admit it, not many love-stories involve single mothers or having sex with the kids upstairs or trying to kiss someone whilst avoiding the tip of their nose because of an angry boil. These things are not traditional love story material, but in my experience not many things are.

It never works out the way you expect it to, does it?

We had sex. Right there, on that night, the saddest night of my life. That night was like cycling to the top of a mountain in fourth gear and then free-wheeling all the way down the other side, making whooping noises and laughing. You know the sort of free-wheeling I mean.

So, sorry, but you appear to have missed the best bit, what with all that time spent telling you about my relationship with the insect world. We've nearly finished now, actually, I talked ants right through the good part. Never mind, just think about the last time you had sex with a man with wolf- brown hang-dog apologetic eyes and just fill in the blanks yourself. If you're a man, and you're not gay, you probably don't want to hear too much about it anyway, so let's just crack on.

I'm lying in his arms afterwards thinking, 'I'm lying in his arms afierwards, I really really am. This is my dream, my fantasy fulfilled. The hating and poisonous hole in my heart has been poured full with warm honey and this is how it feels. I wonder how my boil's holding up.'

That wasn't quite afterwards.

Straight afterwards one of the boys woke up and I had to go and change his nappy and give him juice and a cuddle and try not to think about what a wanton slut I was. The Elephant Man said, 'I'm not an animal, I'm a human being.' Fair enough, I can see his point. But when you're a mother you're not a human being either. Try imagining your Mum loving a shag or fancying the arse off somebody. Go on. She should be cooking your tea, shouldn't she?

See what I mean?

So, I'm in his arms.

'You're so pretty,' he tells me. That's nice. I'm not pretty, but I can see what he means. The firm jaw, the big white teeth, it fools a lot of people.

'You smell like my gran.'

WHAT?

Whatever else I was expecting him to say, this was not it.

'My gran used Avon make-up, too. You smell like her.' He laughs at my expression.

'You don't LOOK like her.'

'Thank fucking God for that. I don't shag like her either.' I'm prone to filthy talk, I apologise. I like to think it makes me racy and sexy and exciting, when it actually just makes me look like a foul- mouthed whore.

'Could you do me a favour, sweetness? Could you take your make-up off before we make love? I'd love to smell your natural skin smell, instead of all that make-up.'

Now my vanity defence systems are on red-alert.

Take my make-up off? I cup my face in my hand and wriggle up on one elbow. His face is beautiful, smooth and peanut brown, as if Tony Hart has just made him out of clay. No finger-prints, isn't it just so magical the way they did that? If I took my make-up off, he would see my acne. He would have sex with me, looking at my acne. I don't want to think how bad my face looks when I'm having sex at the best of times, eyes screwed up and nostrils flaring, let alone all that dipped in a bowl of molten porridge. But one thing he says stands out from all the rest.

'Sweetness.'

He called me 'Sweetness.'

We started at hello and here we are at 'sweetness.'

Wow, this guy is fast.

This guy does nought to relationship in sixty seconds, he should be on Top Gear. Jeremy Clarkson could rev him up

at one end of the track, and they could be shagging the arse off each other by the time they get to the chequered flag.
This is the love cheetah burning it to pick out the weakest member of the herd.
This is the love Kessel Run in less than twelve parsecs.
In my head, Chewbacca powers it up to light speed while Han Solo pokes his head out of a hole in the floor holding a spanner and looking vulnerable.
This is fast.

BRING THE KIDS

It's been a few months now, and we're settling into a sort of a routine. Before, my life was a swirling tomado's eye, imprisoned into stillness in the silent epicentre while the alarmed observer watches it chaotically weaving about. I had the kids, so my life was looking pretty static terms of any other kind of achievement. But kids, fucking hell, there's some movement for you.
There was no pattern, nothing solidly hopeful. Just a destructive tasmanian devil-style craziness. The kids were all over the place, I was all over the place, we were just holding on to life by our finger-tips and closing our eyes. And like I told you, that night, that saddest and happiest night of my life, that was when I nearly went over the edge of the sanity waterfall. But now we have a routine, and I have a glorious beacon to ride towards. Not the hope of getting married or anything, not that, just the knowledge that something wonderful will happen. And knowing exactly when that something wonderful will be. On a particular day, with time skidding me joyfully towards it, I will see Danny. The tall man.
I was so sure, so certain a curtain had come down for me. I didn't expect this.
We have sex three times a week, which is every time I see him. He comes round just before I put the
boys to bed and cooks me dinner, watching from the doorway while I read storybooks as if unsure how deep

into my life he is ready to swim.

We spend two weekends a month together, when the boys are at their father's house, marvelling at the freedom of it all. We dance and we drink and we laugh with witty good-looking friends.

I spend the days in a happy dream, each day afterwards remembering him, and each day beforehand waiting for him, he is perfect. Life is bearable, which is an improvement after everything that happened before Robert Shaw wet himself screaming in Jaws two months ago.

Then one day he says the inevitable.

'Why not bring the kids?'

Why not bring the kids? I'll give you some reasons, while we're on the subj ect. Well, you weren't but I was and who's writing this anyway?

There's this test they do on SAS Survival, a test to see if you're hard enough to be in the SAS. Let me tell you now, any single mother in the world could piss on that test. We do that test eight times a night and still manage to find Darth Vader's lego light sabre at seven in the morning. We do that test all bloody day, while making 'Sunshine' breakfast cereal and drawing round our fucking hands. Any mother, any parent at all who has ever spent every single fucking bloody day of their lives looking after their children has passed that test, so sign me up now, Eddie Stone. Storming the Iranian Embassy? Get a couple of mums in there, we'll do it and get a Tweenies video from out the back of the couch while we're in there.

Am I hard enough? I'm double hard, mate. I'm TRIPLE hard. I'm your Mum.

The test is about maintaining a high-stress position

whilst listening to white noise.

Have you ever slept in a bed with two children under two? The would-be SAS members had to hold out for eight hours. Me, I've been doing it for years.

So, why not bring the kids, eh? A lovely social event, I can imagine how Danny saw it — friends, kids, a happy picture. Gorgeous, sexy, wide-smiled pebble-dashed girlfriend and her cheeky but ultimately well brought up children. Oh, Christ. Oh, Christy Christ. Let me fill in the details, it's a

good bit, and it's also the bit where I meet Ben.

Danny has invited me to a party at his house, just some friends having dinner and a drink. Why not bring the kids? I don't usually agree to things like this, not with the children, and seeing as I usually have the children, well, you can imagine how often I agree to things like this.

But this is the man of my dreams, for God's sake. To be honest, he hasn't taken much of an interest in the kids so far. He's been nice to them, when he happens to appear before they go to bed, but he's never offered to spend any time with them before. They aren't emotionally traumatised by his lack of interest, they don't give a shit. To be completely truthful, they care more about the fact that he has a blue car than the possibility of his finer feelings towards them. When you're two, blue cars are the glorious epitome of human accomplishment, and my boys are no exception. He always gets awkwardly out of his car, long legs tapping blindly for the kerb like a trapped crane fly, but the kids are out of the house like lemmings. Blue car! Blue car! Blue car!

I manage to restrain myself from doing this. Most of the time.

I'm going to go to this party, and I'm taking the boys, but there are a few things preying on my mind.

Firstly, as always, there is the acne. I am staying overnight at Danny's house, but obviously there is going to be no 'washing my face and jumping into bed with boils shining like ripe plums' scenario happening there. Absolutely no. I always leave the cement cemented firmly on, and then wash and re-apply in one desperate ten-minute scramble in the morning with the bathroom door firmly locked. A fellow-acne sufferer once told me that she stayed at a man's house impromptu (never do impromptu with boils, they beg forward planning) and had to improvise in the morning with some talcum powder she found in his cupboard. I can hardly bear to imagine her creeping downstairs, hoping to coax an embryonic relationship into life whilst looking like a badly cooked pancake.

He never phoned her back.

So the boils are covered, so to speak. Then there is the matter of the children. Will they sleep? Will they eat? Will they scream? If I stay up too late I will feel shattered in the morning, but toddlers are no respecters of hangovers. Porridge will have to be made, nappies changed, and they will expect me to be as efficient and energetic as Mary Poppins on fucking acid. In fact, everybody there will expect the Mary Poppins bit, the bastards. None of them have got kids. The reality that sometimes Mary Poppins has the urge to growl 'bugger off' after years of appalling sleepless torture has yet to confront them. I will have to present a front: happy, efficient, sexy, funny and calm. All of these things are in direct opposition to the true nature of my condition. I am a spotty, exhausted, desperate freak. But Danny doesn't know that, and what he doesn't know won't hurt him, even though it might fucking kill me.

'They don't show.' Gemma is staring at me, staring at myself.

I'm looking in the mirror one last time, before I go. Danny's waiting outside in the car, I'm looking in Tone's sister's fish-shaped monstrosity on the kitchen window sill.

'You know that girl who came round? The one from the restaurant? She said she couldn't believe it was you. She didn't recognise you.' Gemma puts her head on one side, feigning innocence, while she gauges the depth of her incision.

The girl from the restaurant last saw me before the acne came back. 'Why didn't she recognise me? Was it the acne?'

Sometimes I just confront things head on, rip that plaster off, get it over with. Funnily enough, I can only confront things which are painful for me, I can't inflict it on someone else. I wish I could, I wish I could, Gemma, you cunt.

'No, no, no,' Gemma is embarrassed now. She can do it slyly, but she's not got the stamina for a full attack.

'I think you've lost weight, that's all.'

'That's okay then. If I thought these spots made me unrecognisable I'd fucking kill myself.' I try to say it lightly, going for black humour, but as usual the bitter truth bites the joke in two. It's almost true, and she knows it. She's bitten off more than she can chew, with me. But she sticks at it.

'Eva's lost weight.'

How the FUCK does she know that?

Sally, right. RIGHT.

For once, I keep quiet. I've got to get the nappies packed and the kid's shoes on and open a huge umbrella in order to fly to Danny's house, I haven't got time to be baited like a sad-eyed bear with all the fight drained out of him. My silence frightens Gemma and she offers my oldest toddler a portion of pasta to take in the car. Even this small offering appeases me, I am so weak for kindness. It still grates on me, irrationally I know, that Gemma and my son share a taste in pasta. How do you think Gemma likes her pasta? Go on, I want you to guess.
Spot on.
Plain. Fucking plain! Who the hell eats plain pasta? Apart from my son, but he's three, he eats lego. 'Where's Danny then?'
That's not Gemma, that's my Dad. Dad comes round a lot, ostensibly just for a quick visit (no tea, it stops you sleeping) but really to make sure I'm okay. I'm only eleven to my Dad, remember? A pre-teen with two kids, a lodger and a mortgage. No wonder he's worried. 'Dad, I'm leaving right now, we're staying at Danny's...'
'With the boys? Good. Good.'
Men have to take an INTEREST IN THE CHILDREN. Any men, any children. My Dad's taken out some pretty firm moral policies with whatever celestial being governs his fortunes, and being good with children is one of them. Especially if they're his grand-children.
'Was that Danny's idea then?'
My Dad scrutinises every word I say and makes accurate judgements about me and my life in the twitch of an eyelid.
'Yes, Danny asked me, he asked me to bring them.'
'Good. Good.'
My Mum stumbles into the kitchen on her cheap plastic

heels. She goes cheap because she's so middle-class she doesn't have to give a shit, not because she's so shit she can't look middle-class. She gives Gemma a cursory smile, but she's not over-polite. Like bullies teaming up in the playground, Mum and I are on the same side on this one.

I look out of the window, I've got to go. I really do have to go. The kids are all over grandad, fuck, I'll never prize them off now, plain pasta in a sandwich box because eldest son won't eat the food, nappies packed, make-up bag packed, I've got to go, I really do have to go.

I can't believe it.

'Mum,' I say, 'I think the dog's crapped in the garden.'

Like God, my Mum hates anything to happen without her full approval.

'She's not due for a poo.'

'Mum, there's shit on my lawn, and I've got to go.'

'Maybe it was a fox' says my Mum, hopefully.

'I'll clean it up anyway,' says Dad, hurrying out. The poor bloke has had to keep his shoes on for thirty years anyway, he's covered for this type of eventuality. When Mum turns the stress counter round to dog shit, Dad is primed to act fast. He's clocked up a few miles on that one, I can tell you. 'Make sure Danny plays with the kids,' says Dad, once the shit has been shovelled and he's washing his hands just a bit too thoroughly.

'I've got to go. I've really, really got to go.'

My Dad rolls up his shirtsleeves tightly and compactly as if the mere thought of a man not taking an INTEREST IN THE KIDS makes him want to cut off the blood supply to his own hands.

'He should be as interested in talking to the kids as he is to you.'

The veins in his arms bulge out, panic-stricken at having

just been so brutally constricted. Shirtsleeves, face, jawline, veins, all tightly packed and pointing at me. I know Danny's being assessed, sized up, considered and judged in accordance to Dad's holy law, I just hope to God Danny doesn't know that too.
Finally, we're in the car. Bags, juice, nappies, pasta and all. Kids strapped in, man of dreams in driver's seat, fantasy scenario just a little skewed.
Danny looks at me quickly.
'You look beautiful sweetheart,' he says.
'So do you,' I reply.
'So,' he says conspiratorially, all knowing smiles and overnight bag-ishness.
'What time do the kids go to bed?'

We drive to Brighton over the Sussex Downs, I love this drive. In my head, it's associated with escape and adventure, flying over the hills with the road snaking away in front all the way to the man of your dreams. Danny's car is tinny, dirty, full of grimy bits of paper and muddy trainers. It's a young childless person's car, like his house. Not that his house is tinny or grimy, it's just a young person's house. He's got this poster of an old woman staring morosely at the camera, with the caption 'drum and bass is my life' underneath. That's a childless person's joke, the bastards, that's childless people saying, 'Look how ridiculous it is to imagine old people having as much wild and incredible fun as we do. We're young, we're sexy, we listen to sexy young music and laugh at the thought of anyone else having their own crap, mediocre concerns.' I'm only eighteen months older than Danny, but I'm on that old lady's side. She might think drum and bass is crap, she might be right.

Danny helps me get the boys out of the car and we go up the five concrete steps to his house. He lives in one of those tall seaside townhouses, but only in the top bit. Unseen strangers come and go mysteriously downstairs, letting agents' billboards go up and down and it exudes the general impression one would usually associate with the word 'basement'.

We go up, up, up, into Danny's top flat, which has a staircase so it's really more of a sort of house. Phil lives here too, to help him pay the rent, and it works out okay. Its a nice feeling, brother and sister, boyfriend and friend, like everything in a tidy circle. Tone and Eva made a circle of two and shut me out, but here I am in a new circle of my own. Why not bring the kids?

There are people already here, laughing, talking, freely getting up and walking about whenever the mood strikes them. I will not be able to do that, so I sit on the floor and prepare myself to look interested in lego whilst making acerbically witty conversation with the childless bastards around me. I divert the children, play with them and answer their questions, I can do it all can't I?

I chat to young lecturers, publicists, good-looking clever people with important things on their minds. The kids need their nappies changing. The kids need juice. The kids need bedtime stories. The kids need mummy, muuummmieee muuuuummmiieeeeeeeee.

The publicists and lecturers melt away.

Why not bring the kids?

I need the toilet, but I know the kids will not sit down here, in this crowded roomful of semi-drunken strangers without me. I want to talk to Phil, but I know the kids will not stay here in this smoky, noisy roomful of looming adults without me. I am gagged, bound, trussed and tied as surely as the chief pervert at a masochist's nautical knots convention. All it does, being here, is act as a constant reminder of what I cannot do. I wish I was at home, in the quiet with a Muppets video and a hot blackcurrant juice and our own quiet bed.

All around me young successful people laugh and drink like the childless, carefree cunts they are. Eccentric types with wacky hats and floppy waist coats, sneering types with scruffy jackets and sharp faces, sincere types with wineglasses and headscarves. Not one of them gives a flying bastard shitting fuck about the woman with the lego. Why would they?

I'm so jealous I could eat my own leg.

Phil is laughing loudly with one of the publicists. She's a good friend Phil, but she doesn't really know how to cope with the more starkly realistic areas of my life. The tide of people washes her up next to me at one point, and as she stares down at me I feel like the old lady in the drum and bass poster. So out of place it's almost comical. Comical to other people maybe. Not to her, she probably preferred bingo, and so what? At least she didn't have to sit in a room full of bastards actually listening to the drum and bass. She had more sense.

'Fancy a game of lego?' I ask Phil. She laughs, like other peoples' social isolation is vaguely amusing, as long as it doesn't impinge on her own sparkling lifestyle.

'I told you, I'm just not interested in your kids,' she says bluntly. 'They bore me.'

Sometimes Phil's beautiful jarring honesty is just jarring. There is no chance I would ever point this out to her, I'm far too fearful and inadequate. But before I can even contemplate her desertion she is suddenly distracted by a middle-class hippy with an expensive leather cap over his dreadlocks and forgets about me. Me and the drum and bass lady lock eyes.

'Don't worry about those cunts,' she says, surprisingly for an old lady. 'Come to the bingo with me. But leave your fucking kids at 'ome, love, I'm too old for all that shit.'

'What am I going to do about my acne?' I ask her. 'Did you get acne during the war?' She pisses herself laughing at that one, her foot shoots out and nearly knocks the 'a' out of the word 'bass' beneath her.

'I'll tell you what love, this music is shit.'

'I agree with you. But what about my spots? What can I do?'

She pulls out a little hip flask and swigs from it before she answers. Her small blue beady eyes assess me, she is so deeply lined with knowledge, there must be something in there for me.

'Just squeeze the fucking thing. Just fucking do it,' she says.

Danny talks briefly to my oldest toddler, but the pull of the party proves too strong and he melts away into the porridge of publicists. I shut my ears to it, all the vibrant excitement of youth all around me, and concentrate on my sons. If I don't they will pull on me, pull on me, pull on me mmmuuummmiiiiieeeeee oh god will you just FUCK OFF.

Oh Christ, did I say that out loud?

No, thank God, I still look like a normal person.

I just haven't slept for a year and a half.

I haven't eaten properly for a week.

Mary Poppins in toddler bloodbath shock headline. I can't do this shit any more.

I read stories to my son until four in the morning, whereupon he falls asleep on the sofa in a confused and exhausted stupor. The youngest wakes up, requires cuddling, cleaning, and re-positioning.

At four-thirty in the morning I am finally a person again, I have about four hours to snatch a fragment of humanity back from the shattering vigil of the night. Danny sees out the last of his guests and we creep under the duvet to make the sort of desperate love that burns at both ends. He is so infinitely tender and beautiful, his chipmunk eyes so kind, his long fingers so very patient, I forget the eight-hour lego vigil and lose myself in the long body of his love. Sex at its best is a form of communication, I think, a kind of physical telepathy. There is wordless understanding there, trust, obviously, and looking into each other's eyes for that truth which only your lover knows.

Later I think, well. The cunt could've at least read them a fucking story.

Why not bring the kids?

I tried to explain it to Phil once, what it's actually like trying to look after small children at a social event. Your own small children I mean, not making faces at your dribbling nephew during some cousin's wedding and feeling so fucking pleased with yourself. Do I swear too much? I'm sorry, but when I feel strongly about a subject I swear too much. As I feel strongly about most subjects, swearing too much is pretty much a constant burden. Just ignore it if you don't like it, I'd do the same for you.

Looking after children is a job. If you're on a payroll, its considered a job. So how come if you're looking after your own children, its nothing but a government money-draining skive?

Here's an analogy. Your children are a job. Like working

at a computer, which constantly demands your attention. In fact, if your attention is diverted for a moment it starts to emit high-pitched beeping noises. So get back to that keyboard. Now get another computer. Two computers, two jobs, two high-pitched beeping noises. Now imagine your working hours. Eight hours? Nine hours?
No such luck. All day and all night. You don't go home from the office, those beeping noises follow you home. In your sleep, in your dreams, while you eat, while you shit. How long is your contract? Years and years and fucking years.
Why not bring the kids?
Because sometimes, just SOMETIMES my patient readership, I just feel like having a day off.
The next morning the kids wake up at a fairly reasonable time, and I make them porridge in Danny's tiny young-person's kitchen. There is only one guest from the night before, he is sitting at the dining-room table and grinning broadly. I suspect he has not slept, but not for the same reasons that I didn't.
'My niece is about his age,' he says in a friendly way, indicating my son.
'She's great. I kept on making faces at her during my cousin's wedding. She was laughing all the way through the ceremony,' he laughs in a nice way, as if he wants me to join in.
'I love playing with kids.' Oh yeah? Where the fuck were you last night, then?
'They don't care, do they? They don't judge you.'
That catches my interest a bit. Why is this bloke so afraid of being judged, anyway? I'm afraid of being judged, but that's because I'm painfully aware of the sad inadequate twat I really am. Is this guy aware of that too? His own

twattishness, I mean, not mine.
'You can make a twat of yourself with kids. They don't care.'
I spoon porridge into the two beeping computers, which temporarily silences them both. They are sitting low on dining room chairs, nostrils balancing on the edge of the table, Action Man trainers swinging to and fro.
'Personally, I'm too tired to enjoy it any more.'
This is too much truth for an introductory comment, and the man squints at me. His small eyes are deep-set and intelligent behind his glasses.
'I think you're a brilliant Mum, you play with your kids. My sister, she doesn't really play with hers that much.'
'I do like playing with them, really. I'm just tired.'
Suddenly, I regret being such a miserable cow. It's the 'brilliant Mum' comment. Like I told you, I'm weak for kindness.
'Did you know, sleep deprivation has actually been used as a form of torture?' I always tell people this.
'Yeah, after a while it can effect your brain and cause depression can't it?' Wow, straight back at me squinty guy.
The kids start to smile at our myopic friend. He does indeed make excellent faces.
I look at him a bit closer, this man who knows about sleep deprivation and depression and feeling like a twat.
'My neice screamed all through my brother's wedding,' he tells me. 'My sister was just too knackered to take her outside. Even the vicar didn't hear the ceremony.' He smiles at me unselfconsciously and jumps up suddenly.
'Do you want a cup of tea? I'll put the kettle on. Shall I get some juice for the boys?'
Again, a small offer of help and kindness wrings out my

tear-ducts like a hanky. That is the first offer of help with the children I have had for over a year. Apart from my parents, when they're not cleaning up dog shit and rolling their sleeves up too tight.

I have never had a husband, so the concept of a man who gets juice and brings it to children is something which for me only exists in my childhood memories. My Dad did it, maybe he was a dying breed. Who knows?

But here is a man, offering juice.

'It's okay, thanks, I'll make it. They're pretty fussy little fuckers.'

I don't mean to sound harsh. I told you, I swear a lot. The kids know that.

Squinty guy smiles at me again. His eyes sum me up. Accurately.

He reminds me of a friend I had at college called John. He used to sum people up pretty accurately, too. He had me taped, he had my number, whatever you call it for knowing what sort of a person someone is. I could see it in his eyes, he bloody KNEW me. Bastard. He loved me, I could see that too. I must ring him sometime.

The man in glasses takes in my scrawny neck, my acne, my general piss-taking bravado wall-papering the cracks in the plaster of my togetherness. He has tiny freckles in the delicate skin under each eye.

'Look, if you feel really bad, why can't someone come with you when you go home? Can't someone come and help you? We should all go.'

This sounds like a glorious utopian vision, all those clever, good-looking, party-loving Brightonites, all madly playing Star Wars Lego so I can put my feet up. Would they fuck.

'We can't,' says Danny, suddenly appearing behind me like

a languid poltergeist and rubbing his palms up and down my upper arms.

'Sorry, sweetheart, but we're going to bust the box this afternoon.' He kisses me and moves me gently to one side to squeeze through into his tiny youthful kitchen. Squinty man looks a bit torn, memories of relatives suffering at weddings clearing skimming across his brain. He's seen kids bugger things up and he wants to help. He feels for me I can see that, but let's face it, 'bust the box', that sounds good. He exhales, letting a thought go, Buhddist-style. I can see which argument is winning, as he turns his small blue eyes to squint at Danny.

'What time does it start?'

HELP ME, OBI WAN

It's still the same day, still the day after the party, and the kids have fallen asleep on the sofa. I have an hour, now, in which to be a person. It's strange, having one hour off in a seventeen-hour merciless day, there's so much living to cram in its almost a relief when they wake up again and I can stop being so conscious of making the most of it. The first ten minutes, that's heaven. The peace, the joy, the possibilities. Every ten minutes of the hour after that is just a downwards spiral of lost time and increasing panic. Then they wake up, and I realise I've done fuck all. Again. Danny, in his clear-skinned unashamed innocence, suggests a bath together. I agree, because what can I say?
The alternative would be to tell him, sorry, but if any water splashes on my face you might suddenly become aware that you are in fact having an intensely sexual relationship with the singing detective. So I agree.
Here we are, in the bath. Hot bath, steam, just the thing for bringing those blood vessels rushing to the surface of your skin and glowing like, well, like a woman with bad acne in a hot bath. Slippery bodies squashed together and wet lips meeting in a kiss. I know all the clichés that need to be fulfilled here, I've been to the cinema, I know what goes on. I just don't look up to the job, and my self-esteem has a nasty habit of reminding me every time I look in the mirror.
I press my face in his wet shoulder, wishing I had long

hair at least. There's nowhere to hide.
'But sweetness, I'm your boyfriend,' says Danny gently, when I tell him. I try for disarming honesty, wide child-like confused eyes, rather than embittered spotty cow. He doesn't tell me which image springs to mind.
'I love you, I don't care if you've got a rash.'
A rash. He can't bring himself to say the word 'acne', that would imply that he had an ugly girlfriend. This is intruding on every aspect of my life, I think to myself. I'm not going to let it spoil my life any more, I'm taking charge, I'm sorting it out.
'Why don't you go to the doctor's if it bothers you that much?'
Right, I fucking will then. I fucking will.
He scratches his cheek with one finger, something he can do without even thinking. Something he can do without accidentally hurting himself, the lucky bastard.
'You could go on the pill at the same time,' he says.

I am in town with the boys, I've got an appointment at the doctor's. Like all tragically blighted types, now I have made my decision all my eggs are stacked up in the doctor basket. Should she tell me 'it's only a few spots', or worse, 'I can't really help you unless I've seen them properly. You'll have to take your make-up off', the basket will crash to the ground in a shower of my shattered hope-eggs, and there will be a close-up on my loose lying lifeless hand. This matters to me.
Doctor's surgeries these days are pretty child-friendly, so the boys fiddle with a few pieces of heavy duty plastic with all the stickers worn off while I wait my turn.
I read posters. Everywhere — tubes, the vet's, waiting-rooms, schools — everywhere there are signs of people

trying to tell you something. Something that was so important to them that they had it PRINTED OUT, and blu-tacked somewhere public. Fuck, you know, you don't do that with your shopping list. That's what makes films about civilisation collapsing so unnerving for me, it's the shots of flapping, torn, never-to-be-read-again posters, human communication made impotent. The city laid waste by nuclear war, that bombed-out french town in Saving Private Ryan. Always the flapping posters. People aren't listening any more, it says, there's nobody left to care.
Well, I'm here, and I'm listening.
My favourite poster when I was a kid was the one warning about rabies at the vet's. My Mum used to take our first beseeching dog there, she would tremble on the table and shit herself all over the thermometer. The dog, not my Mum. The vet had a tracheotomy, so he spoke a bit like Stephen Hawking, which added to the surrealism of the whole thing.
Anyway, this poster was of a huge snarling german shepherd, the dog kind, not a sheep-farmer eating liverwurst, and it was trying to savage a screaming girl. Don't ask me why I liked it, I was nine, I suppose it was the closest I could get to fear adrenalin at that time. I know it made me feel pretty scared, in an excited kind of way. Mum would tell us stories about rabies in her 'red ants' story style, it was nice when she didn't have any beeping things to distract her.
I like fear adrenalin, it feels nice. Some people will say 'why go on fairground rides or watch horror films? It's just not NICE.' They don't get it. They don't get the rush. Dirty sex, cheap dirty nasty sex, that's not nice either, but Christ, what a rush. That's why I was watching Jaws,

it's why I like horror films generally, I can see why some people get addicted to it. I read somewhere about it once, in a feminist book, about football hooligans experiencing the 'pure pleasure' of fear adrenalin. Not that I'd ever be a football hooligan — I mean what if I OFFENDED somebody? — but I can understand that addiction to badness.
I think a lot of angry people aren't really angry about the stuff they think they are, they're just addicted to the rush. If only they would take up extreme sports or something, it would stop them getting road rage and shunting old people into oncoming traffic.
Look, it's just a thought.
I still feel excited when I look at posters, sometimes they can change your life. Somebody is trying to tell you something. I'm looking at one now, 'How to Feel Happier' it says. Okay, good start, there are little captions under simple cartoons. 'Phone a Friend'. Yes, that's true. 'Dance' is an unexpected one. Then my favourite, 'Look after something,' and a picture of a kitten. Look after something, what, something beseeching? Something that always needs to shit? And there I was laughing at my Mum.
Now it looks like she's got it all figured out.
My name is called. This is it, I pick up my egg basket and hope to God the handles hold out.

The doctor is a woman, which is a relief. I don't mind showing a male doctor my fanny, but the secrets of my self-doubts and sadness are things I don't want a man to know. She is in her forties, plump, earnest, kind and intelligent like the nicest of favourite aunties. Even her perm is loosely rolled, puffy and soft like her bedside

manner. The eggs are looking pretty safe so far, I reckon. There are toy fire-engines under the bed, so the boys are briefly occupied. Communal toys in places like this, they always have that look of the flapping posters in fihns about nuclear war and civilised order falling apart, they look like its already happened to them. Those dolls with the hair sprouting out of wide-spaced holes with clothes that have clearly been knitted by one of the receptionists, they're the sort of dolls that will be strewn in the streets as a poignant reminder that there's no-one left to play with them. Fuck knows why those dolls are always there, everybody hates them, you'd've thought they'd all be gone by now.
The kids don't mind the post-armageddon toys, they're not that fussy. I talk to the doctor about HOW I FEEL, and she looks as if she wants to gather me up into the soft folds of her motherly perm. This nearly makes me cry — you know how weak I am for kindness.
'I couldn't come without any make-up on,' I tell her. 'I just couldn't bear for everyone to see it. Can you prescribe anything without actually looking at it?' There, I've waited twelve years to say that. My fragile happiness hangs in the balance.
I've been in pain, on and off, for twelve bastard years.
I've been stare-in-sympathy ugly.
Help me, Obi Wan Kenobi, you're my only hope.
At least Princess Leia had the advantage of a fucking HOOD.
'Of course I can' she says, and my egg basket rejoices at her words.
'I know, it's very hard isn't it? I'll tell you what, I'll put you on the pill. The hormone levels should settle down and after about three months you'll see a difference.'

Danny will be pleased. About the pill thing, I mean. Life just seems to be jigsawing into place today.

'You should drink water as much as possible. That will flush out your system and should make your skin clearer.'

Water? I've got that in the tap.

Has the answer been staring me in the face all this time? Like a fat person opting for the salad option, I feel a little bit better looking already.

The doctor pauses in her prescription-scribbling and looks at me tenderly. I feel like she has such a deep understanding of me already I half expect her to say 'Just squeeze the fucking thing, just fucking do it', but she doesn't. She looks at my boys, and at me, with my Oxfam cardigan and home-cut hair and makes an assessment which is accurate, like squinty man did.

'Spots can be made worse by stress,' she tells me.

Then the prescription is in my hand, and I am walking on air to Boots the Chemists. A face! A face! This piece of paper I'm holding could be the key to a proper face that doesn't hurt, or bleed, or weep horrible moisture from swollen boils. A human face, like those ones you see in adverts. A face that Danny could run one finger gently down the side of. A face that could look up in a moment of tenderness or intimacy and feel it has a perfect right to be there.

This is my face, and I'm getting it back. But first, I have to go to Lidl.

LIDL

Everybody has their own method of dealing with their children in the supermarket, and I would be the first to admit that mine is not a method that would work for everyone. My own philosophy, which does me no public favours, is that children should be allowed the freedom to enjoy themselves most of the time. Why should every damn bloody bastard experience in their short lives be accompanied by shushing and stopping them, pushing or hurrying them, why teach them that life has to be so crap? I like to get inside that world, crouch down to examine squashed fag butts for twenty minutes, or stand on the back seat of a bus waving to drivers behind. Why not?
I want the kids to think 'hey, what I like and want and need is actually important' not 'everything I do is a matter of supreme irritation and utterly ludicrous to boot.'
I want to build their self-esteem, so they can go out into the world confident enough to be good, kind, happy people. Adults with high self-esteem are usually nice individuals.
Unfortunately, toddlers with high self-esteem are generally fuckers of the highest order. If you've always been allowed to stop and do whatever pleases you, you are a contented adult, secure in the knowledge that life is there to be enjoyed.

If you've always been allowed to stop and do whatever pleases you, you are a pain in the fucking arse at two years old, because what pleases a two-year-old is never the most sociable of diversions. Nevertheless, despite the disapproval of almost every other adult I meet, I persist with my philosophy, determined that my boys should feel all the contented feelings of self-worth that I can give them. That is my belief, and I believe it wholeheartedly.

But when I'm out with them, at the shops, and I've got to stand in the bread aisle while they take their shoes off and play hobbits on the lino for half an hour, well, it looks like I just don't give a shit. I always suspect people with quiet, passive toddlers. All that suppressed energy, fuck, that's got to come out somewhere.

So here I am in Lidl, the kids running up and down the aisles.

'This isn't a playground' says one woman, tartly, and although I can't collate enough evidence to be completely certain, I would make a good bet that her mouth is exactly the same shape as her anus. 'No, you're right. You should only ever have fun in a playground' I say loudly.

'Did you hear that kids? Let's have some fucking subservient misery please, you're only allowed half an hour of fun today.'

Sometimes, when I'm shattered and fucked and sleep deprived and still doing my best every fucking day, little comments like the one that anus-mouth has just made make me so angry my hands start to shake. My whole face goes red and hot and I swear too much — but you know that about me by now — and everything goes a little bit fuzzy. Who says a supermarket can't be fun? If it gets on your nerves, tough, deal with it, if there were no children in the world the human race would die out.

Just remember the person you're disapproving of works harder than you've ever worked, all day and all night, and sleeps less than you've ever slept. So if you're in the same camp as arse-face, you can fuck off now. Really. Put this book down and fuck right off.
But I'm sure you're not, you wouldn't have started reading this in the first place if you were.
So here I am, disapproved of, tired and swearing, and trying to buy some german tampons. Everything they sell in Lidl has German labels on it, you never quite know what you're getting, but that's half the fun. You have to work out what's in the pizza by looking at the photo on the front of the box, but I don't care. It's cheap, and it works for me.
Besides, me and Eva used to go to Waitrose, I can't bear all those memories.
The kids stand relatively close by me in the checkout, unusually still in fact, and when we get outside I find out why. My oldest toddler tugs my leg.
'Me poo poo' he says, suggesting an imminent defecation.
'Where darling?' I ask, suspecting trousers. We might just make it to the toilet.
He looks up at me, beseechingly. Christ, I love those little buggers, I really really do.
Then he points. Through the glass doors of the shop, through the whole glass-fronted wall of the shop, I can see anus mouth standing in the queue. About a foot or so to her left is a small brown guinea-pig shaped object, unmistakeably my son's poo.
The moral dilemma of the situation is very great. On the one hand, we are home free. We've left the shop, we can run home making whooping noises and shouting and leave the turd to its own fate. On the other hand, leaving

a human shit in a public place, indoors, that's awful. It's unhygienic. Anus-mouth is registering the turd in slow-motion, which is the best way to register a turd.

Like Bruce Willis in Die Hard, I crouch down and prepare to hit them fast and low. I have a wet wipe in one hand, and in my head Bruce Willis says, 'Why didn't you stop them, John? Because then you'd be dead too, arsehole,' and I dash into the shop.

Its a low dash, giving the queuers barely time to analyse the situation in depth. 'Is that a woman with terrible acne making a low dash to grab a human turd?' they might have asked themselves, had I been slower.

I run, stoop, scoop, and exit before the realisation that there is a shit just inches from their groceries has time to hit them. Actually, it wasn't quite that fast. I'm just so fucking British, I can't help it, I felt the need to introduce myself, be polite, even to a queue of total strangers witnessing my retrieval of some family faeces.

'Oops! Hello! I think that's mine!' I said. 'The bloody kid's done a shit again!'

My Mum would've been proud.

MINEFIELD

We come home on the bus, feeling quite pleased with ourselves. The boys are always relieved to be able to shit at all, considering the standard of my cooking. My philosophies about raising self-esteem and engendering life-long self-worth, I put a lot of energy into that. Cooking, I genuinely don't give a shit. We live on tinned macaroni, baked beans, and that weird pasta with the sauce on the inside that looks like a dog's fanny.

I want to get in and start drinking water straight away. It's the fat girl's salad thing.

I put my key in the lock and feel an uneasy resistance. There is a key in the other side, locking it closed so that even another key can't open the door.

Gemma, you parched bastard, why the hell have you done that?

Our front door is never locked, never. Even at night I sometimes lie in bed and remember its unlocked, and I don't bother to get up. I feel like I'm just taunting fate now, circling it like a school bully, 'Come and get me! Come on! Let's see what else you've got you vindictive bastard!' and I can't be bothered to hide from it any more. I'm reminded, at times like those, of that bit in a Vietnam movie — I can't remember which one but I remember this scene — where a bloke is being forced to walk into a minefield by the Vietcong. He starts running and jumping and screaming 'Come on then! Come on you fuckers!' and for about ten seconds you mentally applaud his bravery in the face of death. Then of course, he gets blown to bits. Well, here I am fate, come on you fuckers! You'd have thought I'd have learned something from that movie.

The upshot of all that is the fact that our front door is never locked. You don't get many Vietcong where I live, but I'm sure they're not the only ones who'd fancy nicking our video. I should be more responsible.

Why is it locked? The kids are sitting in the double buggy, kicking their legs and drinking from bottles. Yes, I KNOW it ruins their teeth for Christ's sake, I'm not trying to win mother of the year, here, I'm setting the scene. I decide to tap on the window, I can't wait much longer to get into my own house.

I pick my way through the huge untameable mass which has grown up in front of the window, I don't know what it is but it throws up those tiny ugly red berries that your Mum always told you not to eat when you were a kid. Not that you were ever going to, they look horrible. I look through the window.

My body registers the shock before my eyes do. I get that shot of cold water up the spine and over the scalp, coupled with the pins and needles hands and the desperate need to poo. Shock is like that, like crying or laughing, your body just does stuff without you telling it too. A girl is bending down in my front room, I can't see her face but I see the two blonde streaks at the front of bean-brown hair, the pale chubby arms, I know I saw it then because I can see it now. And do you know? It gives me the pins and needles just writing about it.

It is Eva.

It is Eva, in my front room.

Eva, who stole my life, the man I loved, everything I fucking had, she is in my house. Right now. So what do I do?
I can't believe this, I can't, but I know I did it because I can see it now. I put my eyes down.
I close them right up and turn my head away. Maybe this is my self-conscious saving me from myself, because this kind of anger is not what I need at this moment, with the kids needing to be fed, with a life needing to be led. There is a shuffling and a clinking behind the front door, and after a long time it opens and Gemma is there looking slightly out of breath.
'You're back early!' she says brightly. She never says anything brightly, for fuck's sake, she's little miss prozac.
I run through the house to the back door. I just want to see, just to gather evidence so to speak. My assumption is correct. The back door is not only unlocked, but slightly open, as if someone wanted to stop any body getting through the front door, but be ready for someone to run out of the back. I wish I'd looked harder through the window, but my eyes wouldn't let me.
'Nah,' they said, 'we don't need this shit now. We've seen enough of this crap to last a lifetime, and if you make us look at any more, we will, we'll get fucking cataracts.'
I can't say anything to Gemma, I can't believe she would do it. Eva is my nightmare, my nemesis. I don't want her to sit in my swivel chair drinking my bloody tea. Gemma knows that. Doesn't she?
I can't say anything to Gemma. I mean what if I'm WRONG? What if I OFFEND somebody? My Dad was pretty lenient when we were kids, but rudeness, shit, we weren't even allowed to shout at the dog.
However beseeching it looked.

I do say one thing though, I have to throw it out there just to get it out of the back of my throat. 'You won't believe this. When I came to the window just then, I thought you were Eva! Yeah! Isn't that mad?'

Gemma smirks with her chin pointing upwards, she's won, whatever point it was.

She doesn't say anything though.

This has happened to me before, not this locked door stuff, I mean my brain just editing what it sees of its own accord. Sometimes I think your brain does that to protect you. Like when my acne's really bad, I'll look at it in a kind of detachment as if it's not real, but just with a scientific excitement, like Tony Robinson finding some Roman battlefield or something. Christ, look at that! Look at it! That's bloody horrible, that is.

The same thing happened on that morning when we all found out about Lady Diana, too. It was about five o'clock and I got up to breastfeed my oldest son, he was only a baby then obviously, and I put on the news.

'That's a bit irresponsible,' I thought to myself, 'anybody watching this would think Lady Diana had just died.'

There was her picture with the two dates underneath it, like they do when someone has just died. 'Why have they done that?' I thought. 'It's a good job I realise that this is just a mock-up of what they would actually do if she was suddenly killed a car crash or something.'

After about ten minutes of wondering whether the BBC were embarking on igniting the most colossal mis-placed public panic since Orson Welles' version of War of the Worlds, it occurred to me that she really was dead. For some reason, my brain gave me a ten-minute window to acclimatise myself to it. Strange.

So, Gemma is sweating a touch and can't seem to speak

but apart from that everything seems normal enough.
'I'm just popping out' she says, after a glass of water.
'See YA'. Even the way she says goodbye sounds like she's got something on me. I bet she goes out the back, I bet she goes out the back.

She goes out the back. Her car is parked out front. My brain shuts down this grille once and for all, refusing to let the anger bubble over and stop me making dog's fanny pasta for tea. Once I've got those fannies on, I tell myself, I'll read her fucking diary.

Maybe it hasn't quite shut down after all.

UNFORGIVABLE

Now I have resolved to do the unforgivable, I feel elated. Its so terrible, this thing I'm about to do, its not really me doing it. It's Tony Robinson's Roman battlefield, its my acne, Christ — look at that! I can hardly believe it myself. That's bloody horrible, that is.

I don't even bother to justify it to myself, I mean, I can't really and I know it. I know it, you know it, lets just fucking do it anyway. Yeah! Come on you fuckers, let's read her diary. I put on a video for the boys, The Muppet Treasure Island, and go upstairs. I don't 'sneak' upstairs, because I don't. I just go there, if I felt furtive enough to sneak about I probably wouldn't be doing this at all. Gemma's bedroom is dark blue, like her moods. It's a pretty adolescent thing to do, paint your bedroom a gloomy colour, and for a moment I feel like pure evil. She's so young! So innocent! Who gives a shit? I want to know the truth, once and for all.

I know where her diary is kept, I don't know how I know it but I do, it's in her bedside cabinet. My hands are shaking now but I can't stop myself, not this far in. Badness is a bit of a black hole in that respect, get to close to the edge and it just sucks you right in. I slide the diary off the other books in there, God knows what shit she's reading, I don't bother to look, and hold it for a minute.

'You've been pushed to the limits here, and I don't blame you,' says my evil side, laying a comforting hand on my shoulder.

'Just read the fucking thing! Just fucking do it!' screams my good side, utterly beside itself with excitement at having absolutely nothing to do.

I open the diary and read a few entries.

'Went for a drink with sally. She's engaged to Pete now, and they look happy.'

'Quite depressed today. Went to work. Boring!'

'Got a new dress for the party at the Fox.'

Christ, even her diary is as dull as shit. I'm starting to resent having sullied my immortal soul to this extent, just for the sake of hearing about her crappy life.

'Elaine is going out with Danny. Will it last?'

Elaine is me. Danny is Danny. What does she mean, 'Will it last?' My anger subsides a bit when I remind myself that I'm the one in the wrong here, if she wonders whether Danny and I will last, well, what business is that of mine? Ten minutes later and I've read the whole thing, the whole damn thing, and not one word about Eva. Things never turn out the way you expect them to, do they?

'I'm glad you came with us, it always helps when you don't fight it,' says my evil side, squeezing my shoulder so hard his talons dig into my collar bone. 'What the bloody buggering pissing fuck did you do THAT for?' screams my good side, suddenly remembering itself now that all the tension has gone out of the moment.

My son creeps in behind me, silencing my ghosts.

'Hello darling!' I say, brightly. I'm sweating a touch, but I can still speak. Just.

'Have you finished your dogs fann — I mean, your pasta? Do you want mummy to come downstairs?' As much as I try to be honest about the stress they have brought into my life, I love those little buggers, I really do. I feel guilty now, being miserable and secretive and evil upstairs when I should be playing lego and helping them eat fanny pasta.

'Michul dun poo on floor.'

Michael is at that crunch age, my youngest toddler, too young to be out of nappies but old enough to take them off.

'Oh dear, let's go and sort out that plop scenario' I say. Sometimes I can't help myself saying completely inappropriate words to the children, like 'scenario', that mean nothing to them, but for some weird reason it keeps me sane.

My oldest son comes forward to look over my shoulder, Action Man trainers clumsily kicking on the carpet.

This is the bit where I tread on that mine. All that 'come and get me you fuckers!' all that, was just bravado. I don't really want confrontation, it scares me. Fate, though, wants to deal me one.

I have a cup of tea on the carpet, the same carpet through which Action Man is wildly traversing. In the same moment that it happens, I can see it's going to happen and I scream 'noooooo!' in slow motion whilst diving floorwards in desperate panic.

Action Man meets tea.

Tea exits cup.

Tea finds new resting-place amongst open pages of diary. Liquid biro snakes down the pages and Gemma's dress-buying and going to work activities are no longer recorded in the annals of posterity. They are no more. Not that anybody gave a toss in the first place.

My social unmasking and humiliation are now surely complete. There is simply no way to explain this, no disclaimer or get-out clause, I will have to do the honourable thing. The only thing, given the circumstances, that anyone could possibly do.

I put the diary away and hope to God she doesn't mention it.

The youngest toddler, my own blonde and autumnal son, has indeed done a poo on the carpet. He obviously didn't feel this was quite enough of a statement about his feelings on the matter of the whole 'ignoring them to read someone else's diary' incident, and has endeavoured to actually start eating some of it as well. He's only a very small toddler, a baby really, but a baby with strangely toxic tastes. He has eaten some of his own poo, wow, that goes beyond disgusting. Fortunately my brain does not give me a ten-minute time delay in accessing this information — my subconscious clearly feels that I can deal with this straight away. I do.

I stick him in the bath, hosing him down from a distance. Our bathroom is a nature reserve for spiders, especially behind the toilet. I'm looking at them now. I should have dealt with the situation when it was just one or two, when it was manageable, now the spider population has spiralled wildly out of control and anything short of just leaving them there would be a terrible massacre. Christ, I can count seventeen without even bending down, and not just those tiny little spiders either. I'm talking about those big spindly house-spiders about an inch and a half across from leg to leg. Not an inch and a half across the body, obviously, this is Sussex, not central America.

The back of the toilet is knitted with spiderwebs. I think this is partly due to reading 'James and the Giant Peach' as a child, I never can kill a spider without feeling like Aunt Spiker. This is something which, if you're familiar with James and the Giant Peach, you'll know is not a good thing. Also, my love of the macabre does extend to watching flies struggle helplessly in spider webs, like Robert Shaw, you know their nemesis is in approach. I can watch a massacre, I just can't bring myself to cause one. Besides, no-one ever wrote a story about a giant housefly befriending a small boy and having it's mother killed tragically by an anorexic auntie.

Static as a screaming girl in a seventies rabies poster, the flies await their end. Are they telling stories to one another as they wait? Comparing scars perhaps? I don't know exactly how sentient a

fly is. I hope not sentient enough to crap themselves.

My youngest son then does the single most revolting thing I have ever seen a human being do in real life, he vomits up his own poo right down himself. So now I'm hosing poo vomit and poo, trying to sing comforting songs without being sick all over the poor little bugger. I love that little bugger, I really do.

A couple of bars into 'Feed the Birds' the phone rings.

Ring ring. Ring ring.

This is another one of those rings, another one of life's little pointers, but I don't know that yet.

I don't even find out who it is because I can't answer it, not with a baby in the bathtub, haven't you guys read those manuals? I get him out of the bath, a bit red-faced but still looking pretty healthy, and get him dressed. I really shouldn't taunt fate with fake bravado, I think to myself, it only results in days like this one.

Downstairs and a bowl of fannies later, the phone rings again.

Ring ring. Ring ring.

I pick it up.

'Hello, is that Sue?'

That's the person on the other end, not me. That's not how I generally answer the phone you know. I don't know anyone called Sue.

'I'm sorry, I don't know anyone called Sue.' I say. I'm nothing if not honest. 'Will I do?' The voice on the other end laughs a bit, a genuine laugh, not that exhaling that people do just to acknowledge the fact you've made an effort. It's a nice laugh, a male laugh, the sort of laugh that sounds as if it wants you to join in.

'Yeah, why not? How are you then?'

Hold on, hold on. There IS something familiar about this voice, come to think of it. Who the hell is it?

'I've just hosed shit-vomit off a baby, and now I'm eating pasta that looks like a dog's fanny,' I say.

I'm not trying to be funny, it's absolutely the plain cold truth, but there's that laugh again.

'The irony of it is,' says the voice, 'that is exactly what I do every Tuesday.'

Now I laugh, wanting the voice to join in. It does.

'We're getting on very well for a wrong number, aren't we?' says the voice. 'Maybe we should make friends. We could tell everybody that was how we met, it'd make a great story'.

But we have met before, I just don't know where.

'I recognise your voice, though,' I tell him. 'I think we know each other. Not that well, obviously, or I'd know who you were already. Who are you?' It feels strange, going through these 'who the hell is THAT?' emotions out loud. But I don't think the voice minds. In fact, the voice is having a whale of a time.

'I'm Ben' says Ben. It takes a minute to trawl through my memory and pull out a Ben.

'I think I know who you are. You're Danny's girlfriend,

aren't you? I think Danny gave me your number in case he was at your house and I needed to talk to him.'

Squinty guy! Of course! The penny drops a good thirty seconds after I hear his name.

'Hello Ben. How are — oh, BEN! The guy after the party!' The recognition comes only fractionally after the 'Hello Ben' bit, but Ben registers my fake memory of his name. I was going to wing it for a bit, and wait for the memory to hit me. I didn't mean for it to hit me out loud. Luckily for me, he seems to enjoy that sort of thing. It makes him laugh, something he seems to do a lot. That reminds me, I must ring John.

I really MUST ring John.

'We could have a conversation now, couldn't we? Now we know who we are.'

'Well, I don't know if I've got time, the kids are here ......' I hate trying to talk on the phone with the kids demanding attention, it makes me feel torn apart. I come off the phone feeling as if my brain has been tied to two social horses galloping off in different directions. I'll just be polite, I think, then I'll say goodbye. I mean, we hardly know each other, what could there possibly be to say? Two hours later I put down the phone, feeling great. I can feel a new thought starting to tug on my consciousness, but I don't quite know what it is. Yet.

ROLE MODELS

I've got to hand it to Gemma, if I'm too British to confront the obvious then she is right there next to me, bowler hat on and taking tea on the lawn. We are gagged and bound by our own inability to cope with it. Thank God.
She hasn't said anything about the diary. Mind you, I haven't said anything about suspecting her of bringing my evil nemesis back into my home and relaying all the secrets of my unhappy life to the enemy, so I'm just as bad. Nearly as bad. Maybe.
I'm on the pill, I'm drinking water, I don't know if it works yet because I've only been doing it for two days. Still, I'm a junkie in rehab, I'm a fat girl with a salad, just doing it makes me feel cleaner. The long-term results seem to be within my grasp, or at least, not pitifully impossible.
I have developed a particularly unpleasant habit, though, as a side-effect of drinking so much water. The trouble with drinking lots of water is, it makes you wee. I've got two toddlers, fanny pasta to boil, shit vomit to hose, I haven't got time to wee. Hence the unpleasant habit. You can skip this bit if you want and go to the next part of the story which is quite funny, and is where everything starts to make some sort of sense. First though, the unpleasant habit. I've started weeing in the children's potty downstairs. Oh God, sorry, don't say 'toooo much information' like that; that's crap now, an over-used cliché, don't say that. I've got to give you that sort of

information, it'll help you get a more rounded picture of me. Make what you will of it, but it's true. I don't do it in front of anybody, just when it's me and the kids, and now I'm drinking so much water my piss looks like Evian anyway.

Go on then, judge me if you will. Come back in three months and see if it's working.

In the meantime, here's a bit of a rant about role models for acne sufferers.

Yeah, role models for acne sufferers. Go on, give me one. You can't, can you? I mean, who is there? You need a role model if you feel you are in some way different from most other people, if you are in some way a little outside the norm.

What? Oh, don't give me that '...ah, but what is normal?' crap. Just don't give me it. You know damn well what normal is, and having a face which is rendered agonising by dint of sporting a host of pus-filled boils does not feel normal. Normal faces, you know, two eyes, a nose, a mouth, skin of a relatively uniform colour. I did three weeks of an A-level psychology course once, not very long I know, but long enough to cover that bit about human beings needing the ability to categorise other human beings and to have categories which we can define as within the 'normal' bracket. If you can't do that, if you can't recognise 'types' and mentally file them in your 'normal' and 'not normal' boxes, there's a name for it. It's called autism. Being able to stereotype is an important part of functioning in society, of being able to cope and predict behaviour. I mean, if a huge tattooed thug with a skin head and a base-ball bat approaches you in a dark alley, what do you think? 'Oh, he looks like a nice young fellow. I bet he'll ask me for a jolly invigorating game of rounders in a minute.' Not that you'd suspect someone of being a mugger just because they had a tattoo, I'm just building up a picture for you. But then, if an old lady with a tray of muffins approached you in an alleyway, would you immediately assume you were going to get mugged? Yes, human beings make assumptions, we have to, it helps us to survive. Why was I talking about making assumptions? Oh yes, I was talking about norms. What is normal? Don't start that again, I've already told you about that. Well, if normal is not you, who else is like that too? Who can you turn to for inspiration?

If you feel defined by something, physical or psychological or whatever particular quirk happens to be your personal bent, you want to know about someone who has worn it with pride.

If you're gay, there're role models.

If you're fat, there're role models.

I'm not going to say who they might be, but if you yourself happen to be gay, or fat, I'm sure you have your own heroes who have achieved great things in spite of or because of the way they happen to be.

And before you mention it, I'm not talking about Victoria Beckham's pebble-dashed foundation cruelly enlarged on the front cover of 'Heat' magazine. What sort of inspiration is that? Oh, great, I can aspire to something which someone famous and beautiful is desperately ashamed of, great. She's not saying, 'Here's my acne, have it. It's me, I'm proud of it. I will do great things spurred on by the unique emotions acquired by the bane I bear. I will let it define and shape me in a way of which I can be proud.'

No, of course she fucking doesn't. She covers it up, rubs in the toothpaste, and presumably wishes to God that she was just like everybody else. Nearly everybody.

When I was sixteen, I found a postcard in the A-level art room — I finished that course by the way — of a Pre-Raphaelite painting called 'Hylas and the Nymphs.' I would stare and stare at that picture, and collected as many as I could find, that bloke's wife who had red hair, the chunky birds strumming their lyres, I loved them all. The beauty they depict, that pure, clean beauty like angel's delight before you put the spoon in, that seemed to say to me, 'THIS is what beauty is, this is the sort of woman to whom gloriously romantic things will happen, this is everything you are not'. Shakespeare's sonnets, as well, became a painful love-affair for me. All that alabaster white skin and lapis lazuli veins on perfect faces, nobody that anybody had ever loved looked anything like me. Who do you turn to?

Stephen fry turned to Homer and Plato. I heard a young comedian on television recently saying he always turned to Stephen Fry. Presumably, somewhere, there is a tortured young artist-to-be who will soon be turning to our young comedian who turned to Stephen Fry. I like that, I like the linear nature of all that support and inspiration. It makes you feel that humanity has some kind of continuity to it, you know, the old resonance thing again. Who did Homer and Plato turn to? God knows, but in ancient Rome, apparently they all loved being a bit gay. Mind you, that springs from their deeply-held belief that women were too inferior to love in any genuine way — so while I applaud their non-homophobic stance, they can also fuck off, the sexist tossers.

I'm less sure who fat people turn to, but whoever it is they always seem pissed off when their idol loses weight. I used to be jealous of fat people, I did, I used to wish I was just fat. Yes, yes, I know its not that easy to put down your knife and fork — or just put down your knife and fuck as that's supposed to do the trick as well — but the fact is that there are absolutes to being fat. If you eat less, the fat will go. Your problem will go!! Fuck, hang that carrot in front of an acne-sufferer and watch that donkey run.

There are no dead-certs in the acne world. There are 'things you can try,' but anything, pills, creams, antibiotics or spunk, it's all just a theory. In six months it might still be there, and there's nothing you can do.

When I was nineteen, I didn't eat chocolate for three years. I washed my face for half an hour a day, until the skin between my fingers went crusty and I had hands like a Skeksis on The Dark Crystal. I used every cream on the market, sometimes all at the same time.

Did it go?

Did it bollocks. Give me my face back, you thieving bastard, don't tell me there's no such thing as normal.

A SORT OF ADDICTION

It's three months later now. Isn't it great how you can do that in stories? I wish I could fast-forward like that in real life, it would cut out all that stuff you know is going to take ages, like grieving or waiting for a bad haircut to grow out.

I've found out a bit more about Ben as well. He rings me every now and then, and he's funny. He hates football and he loves cooking, which is a passion I don't share, as you know. But he LOVES children, a passion which I not only share but which governs every waking moment of my tortured life. He genuinely loves children as well, he's not just saying that to look wacky and unconventional — 'hey I'm a big fun-loving wacky kid' sort of thing. He can talk at length about his nieces, about what they do together and how he plays with them, how they hurt and irritate him, and how much he loves them.

I can tell the real thing from a wacky fun-loving phony. Alarm bells are ringing all over the place for me. What do I do? I can't imagine living without my stolen nights of wolfish love with the elongated man of my dreams. On the other hand, I've got two small children. I'm living a disjointed existence at the moment, I bang my tambourine with the other mums during music session

at toddler group one minute, then have stolen nights of wolfish love the next. It was fun at first, it felt like a pick-me-up after a hard day. Now it feels like an addiction.
No real dangerous side-effects to this one, it's just wearing me out.
I mean, its not the sort of addiction where I'm going to be sleeping on a bare mattress with all my windows boarded up or anything. Not the mugging old ladies for the last fiver in their snap-latch purse kind of addiction, nothing like that.
On the plus side, and you'll never believe it, the spots are actually going. Some days there aren't even any new ones, just the crusty old tops of the old ones. I can deal with crusty old tops, yeah yeah, look a bit red and crusty why don't you, you're dead now — I know it, you know it — you couldn't cut it as a boil, you've got nothing left to throw at me.
Its the new ones I can't stand. Little areas of hardness and pain, biding their time, waiting for the perfect moment. Bastards. I can't stand the waiting.
But its getting better, so I'm going to keep pissing in the potty. Gaudy tulips, they say, are so often raised from dung. Or in this case, piss.
My friends Steve and Phil are round tonight because Danny is doing other stuff. Intimidating other stuff you know, the sort of other stuff that always sounds more interesting than you. Whatever it is, he's doing it tonight. It's got to do with his music, because he's 'really into his music', which so often
sounds like a euphemism for 'needs an excuse to keep you at arms length.' Whatever his reasons, he's doing it tonight.
So here are Steve and Phil, Phil is Danny's sister, the

honest one. Not that he's got another, less honest sister, I was just reminding you who she was. She's great. Phil and Steve are the only people in the world who I would tell about the diary incident, partly to ease my aching conscience, but mainly because now it's all over, I can see it was quite funny. Steve doesn't judge, he's a laugher. Apart from anything else, he's put up with me listening to Tracy Chapman's 'Fast Car' on a loop for the last fifteen years and that alone surely deserves some loyalty in return.

'She does smell funny,' says Phil. I've told her about reading Gemma's diary. I tried to redeem myself in her eyes by explaining about the suspicious smell thing, but I don't think there was any real need. The great thing about some friends is, they don't give a shit.

Steve has brought his CD player round, as I don't have one. This sudden musical freedom makes me light-headed. ANYTHING I want, any song, right now!

'How would you mention it though? I mean, what if you were WRONG? There'd be an atmosphere. You don't want that.' Phil and I see things the same a lot of the time.

'And can you turn this shit off? Its about fifteen years out of date.' Okay, most of the time we see things the same.

'Its Tracy Chapman,' I tell her, feeling a bit protective. This album, this is my theme tune. This is the musical score to the film of my life. Its got it all, passion, anger, love, loss. These things don't have a sell-by-date, it's the human condition. I don't say this out loud, but Phil reads my face.

'Well, its shit. Go out and buy some new music for once. Steve, can you get Elaine some new music?'

'She won't listen to new music,' says Steve. My friends discussing me as if I were a wayward child who has recently gone to bed is a habit we have all fallen into. I don't mind, pathetic really, it makes me feel cared for in a crap kind of way.

'I managed to get her into the Chemical Brothers but she only listens to track three. Its ruined one of my favourite songs, actually.' Pretending to be pissed off with me is another habit my friends have fallen into. At least, I hope they're pretending.

'So, the diary stuff.' I try and change the subject before Phil puts on the sort of music that will get inside my body and rattle my nerves like dry spaghetti. At a club, yes. At home? I'll stick to Tracy. 'I think you should just tell her she's a cunt,' says Steve. Out of the two of them, Steve is the quietest, the shy one who doesn't like crowds. But he's no push over, he just doesn't like crowds. 'But what if she's NOT?' says Phil, echoing my sentiments. 'You can't just throw someone out of your house because they smell funny and say 'See YA' in a way that gets on your nerves.'

Steve shrugs and giggles. He'll back down from any confrontation that doesn't seem worth it. He pushes his glasses up his nose and presses his lips together. He won't tell me what do to or judge me, bless Steve, he won't criticise me. Still, I look at his tight smile and his fingers drumming his tea cup. He's not going to help me out, either.

'Just tell her to get out. You never have to see her again.' Sometimes Steve's practical mind winds me up. Think of it in emotional terms, Steve. It's not that simple.

'And didn't you say once that the council pays the mortgage after you've been back here for nine months? There you go. You can get her out, afford the mortgage, and never have to watch her eating dry cereal again.' Thank God for Steve's practical mind, I shall never doubt you again.

'Thanks, Steve,' I say. I mean it, I really do.

'Cunt' he says. Kind of like a term of endearment, I hope.

'So, are you doing Gemma's hair for her tonight?' I ask Phil. Gemma told me Phil was going to do that, and I feel irrationally jealous. The kind of adolescent irrational friendship jealousy that tears girls apart for most of their school lives. 'But you're MY friend!' I still feel that, but I've learned to keep it to myself.

'Yeah' Phil replies, losing interest in me suddenly and staring at her mobile. I HATE that, I fucking hate that. It's like reading a Mills and Boon novel on honeymoon. For Christ's sake, what are you looking for? Contact, friendship, human communication? I'M RIGHT HERE.

I don't say anything.

'Yeah,' says Phil again, looking up suddenly and grinning. 'I'm doing her hair and make-up, driving her there and charging her a fiver. Well, it's my make-up.'

Phil is MY friend, after all. The nasty, immature, irrational fourteen-year-old in me is pleased about this.

'Steve, can you make the tea? I'm knackered.' I try and wheedle Steve with girlishness sometimes, but that doesn't work. He'll back down from a pointless confrontation, but he's no push over, not Steve.

'God you're a cunt,' he tells me cheerfully, through his tight, uncritical smile.

He still makes the tea, though.

DREAMS

I love getting emails, they're the perfect form of communication. For me, that is. Presumably if you're a dyslexic or something you'd probably prefer the phone. Then again, if you're deaf and you fancy the girl in the post-ofiice, its probably more your cup of tea to write a letter. Hey, it takes all sorts. I know my way isn't the only way, its just the only way I've got. I hate phones, they're too immediate, too pressurised. Say something! Go on! Say something funny, just fucking say it! It makes me nervous, phones. Also you can't see them, the person on the other end, but you you can hear the little exhalations and noises they make, you can get a feel for their mood. It's too difficult to judge, too slippery to negotiate, I'd rather write.

And no sending it off and getting it a week later, either. Its just there, right away, bang bang bang.

Here's your letter, have it. And the reply? Could be but a moment away. All the immediacy without the pressure, perfect. So I've been emailing Ben quite a lot. Like I say, he's funny.

There's one from him now, this very evening. I open it and read the first few lines. Then I read them again. Alarm bells start ringing all over the place, but so does some funky jazz. No, hang on, its not funky jazz. I think it might be Tracy Chapman, 'Baby Can I Hold You Tonight?' God, that woman's got a song for every occasion.

Is this what I think it is? It looks like it, but I'd have to sniff him to make absolutely sure.

The first line that I read is this:

'I dreamt about you last night.'

You what, sorry? I read it again.

'I dreamt about you last night.'

I start to feel a little bit nervous about all this. I mean, he's a friend of my boyfriend for heaven's sake. What is he doing? I hadn't ruled out the possibility that he might be flirting with me, it was fun when it was all understated and secretive. But this? What does he want, some great big falling into his arms thing, some big admission of guilt to Danny? Crumbs, if Danny was the love Kessel Run in twelve parsecs, Ben would have Han Solo watching aghast as the Millenium Falcon is outstripped by his tiny, squinty craft.

I'm not unused to men flirting with me, I know I go on about my spots but they're locked in a continual struggle for facial dominance with the jawbone and the teeth. Some men really like that stuff, that strong features business. It certainly helps draw the eye away from the odd boil or two. I know I'm not pretty, I don't mind, but some blokes have really gone for me in a big way. I'm not being vain, I don't expect it, I'm just saying I don't rule it out either. So when I get a squinty guy who makes me laugh and is interested in my children saying he's been dreaming about me, well, I'm going to assume the obvious.

What sort of dream was it? I read a bit more.

'You were standing on top of a cliff with the wind in your hair, wearing a sari. Have you ever worn one? It suited you. You should get one.'

Now this is getting stranger by the minute. The fact is, I

HAVE worn a sari before, in a play I was in when I was about eighteen, and it DID suit me. How could squinty guy have known that?

And that 'wind in your hair' stuff, that can't be real. My hair is only about three inches long. Any wind in it at all does not have a romantic effect, it just makes it look like a badly dyed fright wig. Which in many ways, I suppose it is.

Now I have a decision to make. Ben has obviously decided to take our innocent, albeit slightly flirtatious, enjoyment of each other's cyber-company to a new level. What do I do? I should tell him to stuff it, say, 'look, your best friend is my fellah, sunshine,' but I don't talk like that for a start. Then there's the terrible but ever-present possibility that I MIGHT BE WRONG. I mean, what if I OFFEND somebody? Christ, what if the poor guy just had a dream about a fucking sari for God's sake? Can't a man dream about a wrap-around fastening-free eastern inspired item of clothing without everyone suspecting him of being about to betray his best friend? What's going on here? The truth of the matter is, I like Ben. He's not handsome, but he's something else, and whatever that something else is, it's better than handsome. He has liver-coloured freckles under his eyes which you can't see most of the time because of his glasses, and a way of coughing before he talks that makes him sound, I don't know, important I suppose. He listens as well, making small listening sounds which matter on the telephone. I hate telephones, but Ben does them well. He has the smallest trace of Yorkshire in his voice, just a tiny glazing, like the sweetness on the crust of a croissant.

I like him a lot.

But there's Danny to consider. And Danny's friendship

with Ben. What to do?

The truth is, I've dreamt about Ben too.

I click 'Reply' and sit down to write, trying to find a middle ground amongst the mental carnage. I go for jocular — if he wasn't flirting, it'll sound like a joke. If he was flirting it'll be a reply.

I write:

'Weird, eh? I dreamt of you too! We were shagging on a pile of laundry at Stanstead airport.'

I'm nothing if not honest.

SMIRK

Its the next morning now, the morning after that email. How did he take it? As a joke, I think. It's still made me think though. I haven't stopped thinking since he sent it. I'd better stop thinking at some point because Tone is coming to pick up the children soon, and they have to be clean and airbrushed to perfection. Tone likes children to be clean. Clean equals well looked after in his book, and maybe its true, but clean can equal never being allowed to just fuck about like normal kids as well. Whatever, he's coming. I still feel touchy about him, I'm still sad, I'm still hurt and jealous. I hate that thing people do, that thing where they hurt you and then when you find it difficult to rebuild your life in the aftermath of all that terrible pain and self-doubt which they have inflicted upon you, they say:
'Oh, get a life!'
I had a fucking life, and you took it.
Anyway.
He's coming, in a minute.
Oh Christ, he's here. Why the hell is he coming through the back garden? I watch him open the gate and walk down the path, fairly normal activities you might imagine, hardly likely to invoke the emotional punch in the diaphragm which I am currently experiencing. But it does, it does make me feel like that, and I can hardly bear it. It's too close to a memory of something else,

something the same but not the same, I can't bear it.

I used to watch him walking down that path when he came home from work, I'd watch his golden autumnal arms swinging and think, he's so beautiful, he's coming home to me.

Now I think, cunt. That's MY garden, you bastard.

But it's too close, it's too ticklish this close to the past. He's not coming home, not today, not ever. I am on my own. I'm okay with being on my own, honestly, I'm fairly self-sufficient, I just don't like life putting up enormous painful banners saying 'You are on your fucking own!' all over the place.

He's not coming home, not today, not ever. That's what his walk down the path says to me. I don't think I'd really thought about it before. This thing I'm doing, watching him walk down the path, this is all over for us. Shit. My hands are shaking.

'The kids ready?' he says awkwardly, standing by the back door like a really pushy garden gnome. 'Yeah. I'll get them.' Our conversations are more or less monosyllabic now. What do you say? Whatever feelings he might have, they didn't involve giving a shit about me, so I try to reciprocate.

He comes into the kitchen now, as if he still lived here or something.

Now that he's here I suddenly realise it's his smell that gets me the most. Maybe professor Winston had a point after all because I can smell where he's been, I can smell someone else. You know when you live with someone, and your smells sort of....combine together, to make a communal smell which is your family and your house and your laundry and just, well, your family smell. This is that smell, but it's only half right.

It's my old family smell with a different family, fuck that's a painful one. It's familiar but disgusting and wrong all at the same time. Like the smell of your favourite dinner left in your nan's underwear drawer for a month. It's just wrong.
That hybrid familiarity makes me feel even sicker, it reminds me of being a kid when you think you see your Mum in the playground but it turns out not to be her. It's the almost-there-ness I can't stand. The not-quite-ness tickle in the brain that really tugs at my throat. It looks like love, but it isn't, it really fucking isn't, and you'd better believe it.
Apart from all that smell thing, I really hate having people I don't trust in my house, you know that. Your house is your safety, its part of you. That's why other people's houses are so fascinating. It's like being inside their brain or something, all the little knick knacks or pictures or whatever. Little pieces of their pasts and their pleasures scattered all over the place like a treasure hunt.
I used to be a cleaner when I was a student, going into other people's houses and vacuuming them for four pounds an hour, you know the sort of thing. It was the wrong job for someone like me, not
that I'm a snooper, its not a furtive pervy thing, it's just a fascination with people's houses. Why do people put those china things on window-sills, why do stacks of paper pile up on the top of kitchen surfaces? Us English are such hoarders. A Japanese house, now that would suit me. Simple, low-down, no knicky knacky Franklin fucking Mint malarky.
So I don't like people I don't trust inside my house, inside my brain, reading my life through my possessions, I don't like it. Tone is here now, doing exactly that. His eyes cover

the crispy pants drying on the radiator, the line of dusty coco-pops against the skirting board. Bastard.

'Look at the state of this place,' he says, quite nastily considering that he's the one who ran off with a teenage girl. You'd think he'd be a bit repentant but he's not. If anything he's nastier.

'Look at the state of you.' He looks at me pretty closely. Great, now he's inside my brain, inside my head, staring at my acne. All my favourite things.

I get the children into their Action Man trainers and start them moving out of the back door. I'm determined not to show him my feelings. Just pretend you don't give a shit, my Dad told me, don't give him the satisfaction of seeing you upset. Besides, it would upset the children. And then he'd go back to his angel-voiced English rose even more convinced he'd done the right thing.

Don't rise to it.

Don't.

'Fuck off, fuck off you fucking cunt,' I hiss through my teeth, 'if you ever come in my fucking house again you cunt I'll stab you to fucking death.'

Our back door is made of glass, so as he shuts it I can see him smirking.

THIS ONE

You can probably tell from all this that I'm not really over it yet. Sorry. I am trying, I really am. Tone thinks I'm still in love with him, he even said once, 'What does Danny think about you carrying on like this?' one time when I started shouting and getting sad. Christ, yes, I know it upsets the children. I'll add guilt to the list, shall I?
But I'm not still in love with him. I'm not sure what it is, it's angriness partly — I hate lies, betrayal, being made to feel jealous and inadequate, who doesn't? But it's other things as well. It's left a taste in my mouth that I can't spit out and that pisses me off. I don't want to be this person, this angry, bitter, ugly person, but I am.
So I have another glass of water.
You're not going to believe this, but it is actually starting to work. The drinking water thing, that is — really starting to work. Did I mention that? The acne is going. Well, not exactly going, but definitely becoming a bit more manageable.
A hundred glorious freedoms are now crowding my imagination. Being able to scratch my face, if it itches, that's a big one. Danny being able to touch my face caressingly in a moment of tenderness, that's a big one too. Swimming! I could go swimming!
At the moment, the concept of my naked face being laid bare before the public is too appalling to contemplate. The actuality of my appearance is between me and my

own dwindling sense of self worth, and no-one else.
Being able to smile and laugh without feeling those lumps of poison in my chin. That would be a joyous liberation. Being able to just have my photo taken, just smile and let it happen like anyone else, without feeling desperately aware that my disfigurment is being captured for future generations to gawp at. Its bad enough that people on my own timeline can witness my misery, let alone those who haven't even been born yet.
Being able to give a blow job without wondering whether the man on the receiving end thinks he has been impaled on a puffer fish. Look at a puffer fish, they look like acne. Honestly, they do. Go and check now, then come back. Go on.
It's not that pleasuring men is my sole purpose in life, I would just like to be able to lose myself in the act of love. Weeping facial sores forbid this.
I'm still weeing on the potty and Gemma is still living here. I'm just filling you in on developments, seems a bit pointless now, actually, because there don't appear to have been any. Gemma hasn't said anything about the diary so she must have chosen to ignore it. Thank God. She's still letting things slip, here and there, things that make me think 'how the fuck does she know that?' but there's always the excuse of Sally. Right.
I need some peace for my mind, some green and pleasant land, some rest between the chaos.
I need space where we can go, and there will be nobody there to judge me. Just me and the children, in the quiet of our own private love.
I phone my Dad and ask him to take me to the garden centre.

I've always loved garden centres. They're such an innocent concept. They serve no other purpose than just to create and sell living things for the sole reason of bringing pleasure to the people who look at them. And it's all ALIVE, real, living, photosynthesising life. Plants, fish, flowers and a couple of smug-looking rabbits in pet's corner. All that life is very reassuring. It must be a primeval thing, you know, to be surrounded by life is a pretty good way of staying alive yourself. It must be some primitive memory of starving to death as a medieval peasant during the mini-ice age or something. I don't mean re-incarnation, come on, you must know me better than that by now. I just mean the sort of memories that pass down through the generational sub-conscious and become instinctive. Like a wild animal's fear of man. Or the Royal family's love for the theatre. Come on, first you have Charles the second knocking off Nell Gwynne, then three hundred years later you have Prince Edward on Its A Knockout with Stuart Hall. There's got to be some connection there, it's my old resonance stuff again, I love listening to the past calling out. It makes me wonder what I'm saying to the future. Judging by my usual standards, I'm probably just an old relic screaming out an incomprehensible load of bollocks.

Whatever the reasons for it may be, I still love garden centres.

My Dad takes us in the car, with his usual beaker of acidic squash and packet of ginger nuts, and we have a fag in the car park while the boys eat their biscuits. Dad is relaxed about smoking in a nineteen-forties way, it's a manly thing to do and it calms your nerves. You're never alone with a fag says my Dad's stance, as he cups his fag like an officer in the trenches and damn well enjoys it.

I smoke like a pursed fish-wife. Whilst my Dad's fag says, 'man having welcome oasis of calm', I feel my fag says, 'would rather spend money on fags than buy the kids any decent clothes.' I hate smoking in public, fags and kids are never happy bedfellows, the whole Mary Poppins thing is indelibly tarnished by the presence of a burning Rothmans. Never mind.

Don't scoff at the choice of ginger-nuts, either, they have a special place in my affections you know. They were my brother's favourite biscuits when we were kids, and I admit, at the time I took this as evidence that he just wasn't hard enough to take on the sheer naked excitement which is, I don't know, a mint club or something. But they grow on you.

My Dad is a ginger-nut kind of man. Not his hair, not that, just that he's brown and crinkled and too brittle to be to everyone's taste. But stick with it, put your trust in McVities, it won't let you down and melt all over the A-Z on the way to the garden centre.

There are massive model dinosaurs at this particular garden centre, the whole place branches off enthusiastically into a 'history of earth made out of papier mâché' extravaganza, then bottlenecks back into ferns and cactuses, before finally ending up with a miniature water mill and a train ride for the kiddies. This may sound like hell on toast to some, but I love this type of stuff. Its so clean, so innocent, just there to be enjoyed. What kind of thought process came up with the idea of combining a garden centre with a papier mâché history tunnel through time, complete with model caveman in a rabbit skin bum bag? Its sheer heaven to me, the mad glory of it, I want to be inside that person's

head. The Walter Raleigh figure, I admit, is a bit of a disappointment, being only made of cardboard and glued into a little stand. But to be honest, once you've ridden the earthquake simulator and seen a tree that's older than Napoleon, any more excitement would probably kill you anyway.
'Get the kids,' says Dad, serious in that serious way Dads have. Nobody under fifty-five could sound like that.
'Bring the bag.' My Dad chucks out little sentences like that, little commands. You do them, believe me.
We go to the foyer which is all creeping vines up stone walls, dinosaurs hiding in plastic undergrowth and birdsong DVDs on endless repeat. A big metal stand full of technicolour leaflets advertising stuff detracts a little from the 'at one with nature' ambience, but I don't care.
Even the leaflets comfort me, speaking as they do of clean and happy things. The whole of Sussex is strewn with stuff to do and leaflets that tell you about it. Clean stuff, green stuff, like the makers thought to themselves, 'well, we've got away from the hustle and bustle of London, let's really make the most of it. But how the hell are we going to let the people know?' Posters, they can be a bit static, but leaflets — they've got a life of their own. They're off! They're anywhere! Go! Go! Go! Any bird, any duck, any guinea-pig living in a public place in Sussex is celebrated on the front of a shiny full-colour leaflet with a map of the premises, folded into thirds.
My love for leaflets almost rivals my love for posters in the same respect — they're little snippets of the bigger story. Somebody, somewhere wants you to know something. That in itself is exciting enough. I do love those ones advertising days out with a map of the place, like a real-life Narnia or Pooh Corner, but the London

Dungeon one had it all. The macabre, maps, a description of their tunnel through time, everything. There was even a cartoon of a criminal being drowned at Traitor's Gate, I was in heaven before I'd even got there.

My Dad pays for the tickets and hands them to me. Actually, he presses them into my hand and for a minute I expect him to say, 'Go! Just go! Take the rest of the platoon and fall back!' but he doesn't.

'I'm going for a pee,' is what he actually says. But it sounds important, coming from Dad.

We don't bother picking up a leaflet for the papier mâché time tunnel any more, Dad and I have traversed this well-trodden path many times. We know what works — half an hour on the earthquake simulator, skip past the pterodactyls (don't press the button — it's far too loud for the little ones) and then running through the maze of cactus-lined pathways to the giant carp in the ornamental gardens. The only thing Dad insists on is stopping at the model of a medieval Cathedral. He likes to stare at it a lot. I know what he's doing, he's standing on the precipice of time looking down a thousand years of brick work. He's giving himself mortality vertigo, that's what he's doing, just for the hell of it. I know this because I do it too. I'll really try to understand the concept of death until my heart starts to leap and I have to read a book about guinea-pig keeping or something, just to get my head in perspective. Just thinking about all those people who built the fucking thing, dead a thousand years and staying dead for thousands more, that's mortality vertigo. We're too high up the evolutionary chain, it's not healthy to think thoughts like this.

Then it strikes me, right there by the miniature watermill.

The kids are running about pressing buttons and setting off foghorns and I feel my eyes start to do that burning thing they do.

I'm here, thinking about leaflets, WITH MY DAD.

My Dad, not Danny. I don't have a partner, I have a dirty secret.

Danny's not here and he never will be. If he wanted to take my kids through a papier mâché tunnel through time, well, he would have done it by now. Fuck, he would have SUGGESTED it.

He would have said, 'Fuck all this drinking and screwing on your days off, I really want to find out about the stuff that matters to you,' but he never has.

He'll never flick through a leaflet for the Wetland and Wildfowl trust and think 'hhmm...bogs and ducks, sounds like fun.'. He'll always be the late-night secret, never the green and glorious daytime. I start crying by a three-foot-high light house with working foghorn, watching the kids chucking bits of food to mind-bogglingly enormous fish.

That is what it comes down to.

This, my love for garden centres and mind-bogglingly enormous fish is our separating line. The bastard probably doesn't even like ginger-nuts. The kids, they can live in this world, but they can't live in his. And I'm not moving worlds, not away from the children, not for anyone. I don't care if it's fucking Narnia. So that's it then, that is really it. Separated by one huge fucking mother of a carp.

It gives me pins and needles just looking at it.

Dad sees me crying. He doesn't say anything, not because he's embarrassed, but he just thinks words get in the way most of the time. They're pretty clumsy things, words, they don't get the job done for Dad. He prefers to express himself through thirty years of dedication. It worked for me, it works for my Mum, and presumably it must work for the ginger-nuts as well, because they're still fucking here.

He finishes his biscuit and lights a fag, snapping the lighter closed quickly so as not to excite any German sniper fire. He was only a baby during the war, but that aura of time still kind of hangs around him.

'Dump this Danny,' he says, not unkindly.

'I think its time to get rid of this one.'

Line up on the fire step boys, officer Dad in charge.

'I don't want to be on my fucking own,' I tell him. Dad doesn't really like swearing, but he's tactfiul. He smokes his fag like a Chinese sage at the last supper on Earth. So, what have we learned throughout the millenia of humanity's suffering and pain?

'He's not interested in the kids, is he?' he points out. 'He's not the man for you.'

All my dreams, shattered by the sledgehammer of truth. Thanks Dad. Yeah, cheers for that. Send me a postcard from the Isle of Fucking Pessimism.

'Don't worry about it,' he says, quite cheerfully considering the crying daughter and the fog-horning, fish-feeding grandchildren. Dad loves to be the calm in the chaos.

'I'll tell you when the right man comes along. Just don't do anything till then.' Dad is grinning now, he's got all the answers but he's not telling.

'What do I do now then?' I ask him. I really really ask him. I expect him to have an answer, and it had better be a good one. Dad has a long drag on his fag, thinking.

His past, my past, the same questions, the same jaw-bone,

what is calling to him now? He has thirty years on me, come on Dad, this had better be good.
'Have a ginger-nut,' he says.

A CAT IS JUST A CAT

I'm in the post-office. All that garden centre realisation stuff, that was weeks ago, I'm still trying to ignore it. Yeah, yeah, so I chanced upon a fundamental truth about my life by a miniature light-house, so what? Bollocks to it, I'm going to carry on as if nothing has happened. The sex is better this way. Maybe I like dirty secrets, who knows?
Okay, so we both know the truth, but I'm going to live for the moment for a while. Just because you know you're in Narnia, it doesn't mean you have to go leaping back out of the wardrobe, does it? You can hang about for a bit, meet a few beavers, check out Cair Paravel. Christ, I'm just trying to enjoy life here.
So Danny was round last night. Yeah, we did. I'm not going through all that again, trying to describe it to you, but rest assured it was great. But the morning still has to be coped with, and this morning I'm in the post office. Buzz Lightyear is with us also, hurling himself periodically to the ground. I'm trying to collect my parcel whilst being badgered by two satanic dwarves armed with plastic Disney characters, but I'm in a cheerful mood.
Ben has sent me a present through the post.
I feel guilty getting pins and needles over this one, but here it is.
Ben has sent me a present, and I'm getting it right now.
The woman's in the back, now, getting it for me.

He's been thinking about me, and buying me things. Fuck dreaming about me in a sari, surely this says it all? Depends what it is. Maybe its a joke present, a fake turd or something. I'll know when I see it. I mean, I'll know what sort of present it is. Is it a 'Hey, this is a laugh isn't it?' present, or a 'Look, I'd rather fuck the arse off you but I'm too shy to say' present?
Here she comes, she's coming now.
Fucking hell.

You want to know what it is, don't you?
I don't blame you, thirty seconds ago I did too. Now I know and I still can't believe it. It is a CD playing ghetto blaster, a huge silver one, and I can't believe it. At least three things are now working in tandem inside my head. A few weeks ago, I mentioned that I had nothing to listen to my CDs on. He listened. Not only did he listen, he cared. And not only did he listen, and care, he also did something about it. So here it is. It may as well have, 'I wish to entice you away from your current boyfriend as soon as possible and to hell with the life-long bonds of friendship. Fuck, that'll sort itself out,' written on the letter inside. But it doesn't. The note says, 'You said you didn't have anything to listen to your CDs on. Now you do. Listen away, groovy lady.' I sit in the post-office, staring at my parcel until the children start to take an interest.
'Have you got a present mummy?' says my oldest.
'Yeah, look! It's huge! Lucky mummy!' I say, reflecting on the other context in which I have had cause to say that to myself in the last few months. Except, maybe I don't always think of myself as 'mummy'. Not in some circumstances, anyway.

On the way home we stop at the pet shop for guinea-pig food. I love animals, I really do, but I lack that absurd sentimentality which some people seem to feel about their pets. If civilization collapses, those little boys will be first in the pot, and I'm not talking about the kids.

Guinea-pigs are cute, they squeak and stuff, but they haven't got personalities.

'Oh, they've all got their own little personalities,' people will say about their pets.

No, they fucking haven't. They eat and shit and die. The only personalities they have are imposed on them by us, to try and make something vaguely human out of their eating and shitting and dying. They're animals. Alive, yes, its true. I would never wish them pain. But I would never describe a rabbit as 'cheeky'. Only tossers do that.

These thoughts are crowding into my brain because the woman in front of me in the queue is talking to the pet shop man. He's a strange, skinny, seedy little man. He looks like he keeps animals because he escaped out of his cage once and enjoys the fact that they can't do the same. 'They all have their own little personalities' says the woman in front. See, I told you.

'Ringo, he's such a cheeky monkey. They're all different, aren't they?' This woman doesn't talk, she simpers. Then the pet shop man says something unexpected.

'A cat is just a cat,' he says, ruthlessly. 'It's just an animal. I don't think there's really any difference between them.' Simpering woman and I are agog. This is so glaringly true, so obvious, but so cruelly unforgiving that for a moment I admire his refusal to ingratiate. Christ, I could never do that. He's a strange little man, thin hair over a thin mask of pleasantry. I think that move was deliberate, he's enjoying the look on her face when he doesn't play ball.

I wonder if, when he was at school, he found it hard to make friends.

I'm with him all the way, but I don't say it. If I did, I'd find it hard to make friends too.

The simpering woman stares at him for a moment.

'Well, if I don't receive sympathy for my gibberingly sentimental ideas in your shop, I shall take my custom elsewhere,' her eyes seem to say. Out loud, of course, she says, 'Well, I don't know, maybe...' her mouth just ad-libs while her brain panics. She takes her change and leaves with her cat food, for cats who have been unmasked as the unthinking slaves to instinct they really are. I wonder if she lives with the drum and bass lady. Nah, drum and bass lady has spirit, she'd never put up with that shit.

I look closer at the picture seedy pet man has on his wall. It's of him, cuddling a rabbit. The pose says 'rabbits are my life', but I look at the eyes. The eyes say 'look, it's only a fucking rabbit'.

This is interesting. I decide to ingratiate myself to him, I'm good at ingratiating myself to others, it's a talent I have. I sub-consciously adopt some of their characteristics and mannerisms to make my own personality seem more palatable, I do it without even thinking.

I go up to the counter.

'I need some food for my guinea-pigs, poor brainless little bastards that they are,' I say.

There is a silence, during which I consider simpering. But I think it's too late.

The poor bloke looks fucking horrified.

I take my change and leave, as socially inadequate as a simpering woman's cats. It is then that I notice who is

standing behind me.
The couple who run the toddler group at the local church smile at me supportively. Okay, maybe they're not ruthless seekers after personal truth, but they're kind. As I leave I hear her say to him,
'……you can tell he loves those rabbits'.

IT'S NOT WORKING

We go home on the bus and put 'Brown Eyed Girl' on full blast as soon as we get in. Gemma is there, cooking pasta which will be made, cooked, eaten and digested without ever having felt the luxury of a sauce.
'Hi YA' she says slyly. She's tipped the washing-up bowl sideways again, I fucking HATE that, I really do. I put it flat in the sink, the way it was made to go, and have a sudden rush of courage to the head. Don't ask me what it is, maybe it's the knowledge that somebody is thinking about me, caring about me, somebody other than my Dad. Not that my Dad's not important, it's just that, well, I don't feel it's a particular credit to my credentials, just because my Dad loves me. Parenthood is such a thankless task. You just can't appreciate having good ones unless you don't, and then you'd be too busy becoming a screwed-up anti-social ball of human misery due to the lack of good parents to notice anyway.
Being a mother is a bit like being oxygen in that respect, I think. You never realise how much you need it until you're gasping for breath and turning blue with a chip stuck in the back of your throat. You just have to BE THERE, but don't expect anyone to notice.
So, somebody cares about me. This is a kind of armour for the conversational fencing match ahead. 'Gemma,' I say, 'I'm really sorry' (I'm not, I'm not, I'm just too fucking weak to confront issues without taking the sting out of

it. File down the argument's bull horns, rub vaseline in its eyes, anything, just don't gore me to death. Please. This stuff frightens the hell out of me. Call it Britishness if you like. Yeah, I'd prefer that actually.) 'But I don't think it's working, you living here. We're just..... getting under each other's feet' (tell her about Eva, tell her! Tell her! My good side loves watching me squirm, it likes to watch the action from a distance. Tell her you know she's friends with Eva, go on! Tell her to PISS OFF!)

'And.....the truth is....the boys really need their own bedroom now.' This is my ace card, the one I kept in reserve to play when I needed it. I'm not going to tell her how much I hate her secretiveness, her slyness, the way she says 'see YA' and her weird smell. I can't bear all this.

'You're right,' Gemma tells me, and then unexpectedly, 'I should have helped you more with the kids. I haven't been very supportive. It's been a dificult time for me'.

Even though I hate it when people say that, that 'difficult time for me' thing, when their whole life is clearly going to be defined so as to prevent anyone calling them to book for their selfish behaviour, or any shit they do, it touches me. After all, what has she really done wrong? Maybe I'm just a mad bitch. I'm weak for kindness, weak for apologies too. In this scenario, I am the conversational equivalent of the first little pig's straw house. Shit.

'We should have helped each other,' I say.

Fuck, will she take that? Even I think it sounded crap, and I said it.

'You're right though,' she drones, 'I'll move out. It's pretty harsh trying to get any sleep at night anyway, with the kids up all the time. It's been a difficult time.'

OKAY, now she can piss off. Difficult time? Having to hear another person enduring the misery of months of

sleepless agony. My heart fucking goes out to her. Don't tell me that shit, sweetheart, go and tell an 'Auschwitz' survivor how much you cried when you watched Schindler's List. See how much sympathy you get.
Still, at least she's going.
There is a knock at the door. Gemma looks at me, as if in the last fifteen seconds the door and any answering of it has become the province of myself alone. Her look says 'you asked me to move out, you can answer the fiicking door.' Fair enough. I answer the door.
It's Danny.
'I thought it's time I spent a bit more time with you and the kids,' he says, ducking his head low to get into the house. At six feet seven, he has a constant light-bulb shaped bruise on his temple.
I am now truly touched.
He has made an effort, taken the time, thought about me and the children, and bloody well pulled his finger out, as my Mum would put it. He's come to see me in the green and glorious daytime, and I am so weak, weak, weak for this kindness I throw my arms around him.
'I'm so glad you're here,' I tell him. 'You must have had a premonition we were going to feed the ducks this afternoon. I hope you've got your pace maker, it gets pretty racy out there.'
I'm making light of it, but it means the world to me and more. This is a new dimension, and he knows it. Danny sees my face, and sees just how much deeper into the love quagmire he's just dived, poor fucker. Now he's scrabbling, scrabbling to get out again. Pull back! Pull back! His troops are given the order to retreat, and in his eyes I can see them running for the bloody hills. 'Yeah, well, I had to visit my Mum anyway. I was just driving

past and I thought, why not? I can't stay long though, I'm doing my music stuff tonight, sweetheart.'
In my head, my Dad puffs on his fag and looks at me intently.
It's not just the air-raid siren making him frown.

I don't tell Danny about the ghetto blaster, I'm not sure what Ben meant by it but I'd rather work it out on my own. Danny knows we've become friends, he knows we have this phone and email thing going on, and he thinks it's great. Damn these bloody hippies, why does everything have to be so laid back?
I'm not laid back, as a person, not even remotely. I'm bolt upright, rigid as a dining room chair and less upholstered. But even hippies are still just men underneath. Even the most genuine hippy, loving everybody and sincerely wanting friendship and truth and love and whatever shit they want, even they still fancy a shag. Surely. Because Danny and Ben are hippies, sort of. Not the long-haired sixties kind, painting flowers on their faces and listening to John Lennon, but they're hippies none the less. They tell each other they love each other, and hug male friends. Okay, sometimes they DO listen to John Lennon, but Christ, the man was good.
So I don't tell Danny. He may be a hippy, but I'm not. The kids are eating tinned macaroni cheese with extra cheese, for protein. I'm better at stories than I am at nutrition and it shows. They're skinny, but my God, they've got a good attention span. A two-hour film at two years old? No problem. I know adults who can't concentrate that long. Bloody hell, Phil can't even get through a conversation without texting somebody. For a conversation. She has to have two or three on the go or presumably her brain

would simply shut down.

Danny waits for me to wash up the dinner stuff, and Gemma stares at him. He is worth staring at.

'Going OUT?' she asks, significantly. She has to say things significantly, otherwise nothing she said would have any worth at all. I think she's aware of that. Christ, I should stop being such a bitch. She's okay. Really, she's Okay. It's just me.

'We're going to feed the ducks,' I say, gesturing towards the bread with a soapy elbow.

'Oh,' she replies, pointlessly. She's got the phone in her hand.

Why? Why doesn't she make the call and get it over with? She taps the phone on her leg.

'Going soon?'

'I'm just getting the ginger-nuts,' I say brightly. Then, to Danny 'Let's really make a day of it, you know, take some ginger-nuts and everything.'

I don't need to tell you his reaction to that one.

BOGS AND DUCKS

Part of me is normally reluctant to have others along with me while I care for the children. Looking after your kids is hard work, physical work, stressful work, they ask questions all the time. You wouldn't invite all your mates along to the office would you? I can't stand people trying to gossip into my ear while I sort out Han Solo's light sabre to make it stay in Han Solo's hand (it won't, it keeps falling out, fucking thing). It sounds small to you, but if it prolongs the amount of time between high—pitched discontented noises, it's worth it. It's one more thing that might keep your mental faculties operating for long enough to raise your children to adulthood.
I can't stand being talked at while I work.
I find taking friends with me when I'm out with the kids less like pushing the same heavy cart up a hill together, and more like trying to run a three-legged race at different speeds with an invisible rope. Your mate is getting bored, the kids want to stare at a crisp packet, you feel you need to hurry them up, the kids resent you and you resent your mate.
I can't stand it, I just can't stand it.
So you really would have thought I would have known better.

We drive to the duck pond in the car, it's not far, so the fact that the toddlers are strapped utterly illegally into the backseat doesn't make me feel too guilty. Now Danny has made good his disclaimer, he's fidgeting to get away, I can tell. He wishes he hadn't come. I can tell that because he's quiet and monosyllabic now, probably resenting every second the music world is being deprived of his creative exertions in favour of throwing bread to wildfowl.

Actually, I'll tell him about the wildfowl. I'll try it, why not? Like a sort of litmus test of suitability — if he turns yellow, he's neutral.

Or jaundiced.

'I've joined the Wetland and Wildfowl trust,' I tell him, by way of explanation. 'Look at this leaflet. It's got a map, it looks nice.'

'Bogs and ducks. Sounds like fun,' he says, not sincerely.

There's more than one huge mother of a carp between us, but I'm going to make the most of today. I want it to work, I really really want it to work, far more than I want to be rehabilitated back into reality.

His car smells metallic and uncomfortable. He drives fast, jerking round corners in a way that jostles you inside that tinny metallic little seat. I used to love him driving fast, it's sexy in a James Dean kind of way....oh, right.

Yes, I see what you mean.

Well, the excitement's worn off now, now the kids are in the back. I just want him to have a sensible blanket and a thermos, not an empty fag packet and a ticket to Glastonbury. I feel further away from him, in his car, inside his life which is so far away from mine, than I have ever felt. I have a ginger-nut to force down the lump in the throat.

I look in the side-mirror of the car. I don't know what they're called for God's sake, I don't drive.

Those little mirrors that stick out from the side, you

know the ones. My face looks smooth now, just the odd crusty bit here and there. Just two months ago I had a face like one of those bubbling hot springs that arctic monkeys go in, so I don't mind. A few crusty bits I can handle. I can smile without an agonising reminder of my own ugliness, I don't mind. Maybe its the pathetic fallacy again, but Danny's enthusiasm seems to be dying with the acne. The smoother I get, the further away he is. Maybe his love is just sliding right off the smooth contours of my own face. I don't think he's got a thing for spotty birds or anything, I think its just timing, he's got to make a decision about me soon. It's not a hot flush of new romance any more, I'm looking for a long-termer and he knows it.

Christ, please let this work.

'I didn't really intend to come on an outing or anything. I'm meeting John this afternoon to go through some new tunes.'

I know creative people have their own jargon, and that it describes something really sincere and important to them. But why does it have to make you sound like such a tosser?

I'm desperate to say, 'Oooh, cool, yeah, groovy tunes baby,' and wave two fingers around in a peace symbol, just so desperate you wouldn't believe it.

But I can't, I mustn't.

I must take him seriously, as seriously as he takes his music. I find it difficult to take things seriously, mainly because I have quite a depressive streak anyway, prone to bouts of bleakness which you may have noticed. If I stopped taking the piss, well, the brakes would be off and I'd just slide right on down misery hill all the way to the bottom. Slowly. Not fast or anything. That might inject

some fun into it. The descent into sadness is slow but sure. What's at the bottom of misery hill?
Dry toast crumbs, I reckon.
We get to the common, where the duck pond is, and the boys climb out of the car. Shall we take the buggy? Nah, fuck it. An apocalyptic decision, in retrospect.
Halfway round the pond, my oldest toddler wants to be carried. I'm already carrying the youngest and Danny has a bad back. I don't take the piss out of that, either. Even when I'm carrying two toddlers round a huge man-made area of semi-natural beauty and my arms are going to drop off. 'Can you just carry Jake to the car?' I ask Danny. I hate asking for stuff, I hate it, but my fingers are currently clasped together so tightly and enduring so much strain that they have bulged out in a mass of purple and red sausages beneath my children's perched little bottoms. My hands are a Fred Quimby cartoon, soon the ends will explode only to be perfectly normal again in the next shot. Unfortunately, I don't have another shot, not at this. 'Sweets, I've got a bad back,' Danny replies, and then the obvious. 'Just make him walk.'
Sometimes people without children suggest stuff they think is helpful. I've got a word of advice. Don't.
'He should learn he can't get his own way all the time.' Danny is so sure of himself. I am less sure, even though I know the truth and he doesn't. The truth is this:
I have had screaming, sleepless nights for a long time now. Lonely nights, nights where it is physical agony not to lay down and rest. My hands shake periodically, something I conceal by holding stuff tightly. My eyes water with tiredness pretty much constantly. One more high-pitched noise could send me spiralling into screaming madness, and here is Danny, demanding that

I listen to just a little bit more. Take on another fight, another screaming match. I've had enough, I've had e-fucking-nough, and nobody gives a fucking shit.
Fuck your bad back, you bastard.
I don't say this, I'm too weak. He might dump me, I'd be alone.
Danny compromises eventually and carries the smaller toddler, but won't talk to me all the way back to the car. I've been weak, in his opinion. He's right, but not how he thinks. My small son plays happily with the elephant pendant around Danny's neck, he loves it for some reason. I am momentarily reminded of the time the trunk hooked itself up my nostril when we were having sex
and gave me a nosebleed. I don't tell my son this story, I have some standards, you know.
Danny once said to me, 'Don't you hate it when you have to get up in the night to go to the toilet? You just can't get comfortable again,' which goes some way towards explaining just how little insight he has into my situation. I don't mind getting up to go to the toilet. Its getting up to stagger around producing drinks and clean nappies and Toy Story figures in the middle of the night that I can't take. Being forced upright even though it makes you feel like vomitting, every hour, on the hour.
Taking a piss? I can cope with that. Jump back into bed, nice and warm, lovely jubbly.
When we get to the car he says:
'I can see things more clearly than you because I'm outside the situation. You're too close to see what to do.'
Too close? I'm so close I'm suffocating, mate.
'You should take my advice sometimes, it would make life easier.'
No, you should help me sometimes, THAT would make

my life easier.
I don't say that. I am weak, he's right.
This is all wrong. Poor bastard, he doesn't fit into this life. He wants everything to be solvable, sort- out-able, like it is in his life. He can't cope with just having to cope with it. He's squeezed into the role like a Japanese Geisha, somebody take the bones out of that poor bastard's feet, it's too tight in there.
He doesn't need an innocent escape from his life, his life is great. He doesn't need a moment just to stare at a giant fish and take stock. He doesn't need to create little moments of time which exist outside reality, tiny other worlds of leaflets and animals and innocence, just to stop him feeling like the constant demands for Star Wars Lego are going to send him over the fucking edge. His whole life belongs to him, he doesn't have to snatch any of it back. Bastard.
It's the old maxim, 'one man's innocent escape is another man's bogs and ducks.'
Okay, I made that up. But it makes sense.
Danny sighs and takes my hand. He may not understand me, but he's gentle. He doesn't know he's hurt me. He's like a child who lashes out and then wants a cuddle and a glass of hot juice. He wants to make things better.
'Are you free this weekend sweetheart? I want to show you off at a party on Saturday.'
Nah, that makes me feel fucking worse.

GOING POTTY

I'm still drinking loads of water, still pissing a lot. Christ, its getting out of hand, this pissing. Still, my face is so smooth it gives me pins and needles just looking at it. I've got a new face, and it's the best Christmas ever. I look okay. That's great.
Back to the pissing, you won't believe how much I piss. I am going to that party, by the way. I want to show me off too. But to look okay, I have to endure the constant pissing. It is starting to leave me vulnerable to humiliation, darting furtively behind bushes and trees all the time.
We are watching videos, it is a sunny morning. By 'we' I mean, the kids and me, not Danny and me. The kids and me are watching videos, and we're quite contented.
It's the Muppet Treasure Island, which only improves upon repeated Viewing. The sixth or seventh time you see it you start noticing all the things the rats are doing in the background. I love it. Watch it, and watch the rats in the background, it's a whole movie right there behind the action. We're doing a jigsaw too, a big number thing with train carriages and animals and stuff. Like the jigsaw manufacturer had just tried to cram every cliché of children's educational play into one puzzle. Animals! Numbers! Trains! Wheels! Fine-motor-skills! Cram it all fucking in there and spread it all over the sitting room floor, why not.

I'm pretty happy doing all this, I feel okay, I look okay, I'm pretty happy just now.
I need a piss.
I've already asked you not to judge me for this one. I do the laundry, I change the bedsheets, I'm by and large a fairly clean and attentive mother. But I'm knackered. I haven't had more than an hour's unbroken sleep for over a year. Running upstairs to pee every twenty five minutes is not an option for me, my body simply does not contain the energy for it after nothing but a bowl of hurried weetabix and a ginger-nut. Eat more? Yes, I could eat more, thank you for your input.
Why don't you come round and fucking cook it for me?
I'm knackered, too knackered to cook, because I don't sleep, too knackered to piss straight because I don't eat. That's having kids for you. I'm not trying to pull a big 'poor me' thing, I'm just trying to excuse myself in your eyes because what happened this morning is my own bloody fault.
I need a piss.
The potty is right there, in the sitting-room, ready for action. I'm in a flimsy nightie arrangement, mainly because when you've been dumped for a teenage girl you don't want to look in the mirror every night and think, 'He was right, you know. His only alternative to that teenage girl was a character from Last of the Summer Wine.'
So sexy nightwear it is. Tone may never see it, but I know I'm wearing it. Christ I'm a sad bastard.
I flip the nightie up a bit, and perch on the potty. What the hell, at least the kids will have a role model.
Then I see a face. A face in the very last place I would ever want to see one at a moment like this. At the window.

The fucking window!

There is a face at the window.

It is grinning widely, smiling and waving in a friendly fashion. It's the bloody window-cleaner. Why does the window-cleaner always feel it acceptable to just peer in through the window without the slightest warning or advance indication of his arrival? Christ, someone could be peeing on a potty or something.

The shock jolts me into action. 'Do something! Do something! You've been caught out doing something wrong!' scream my adrenalin glands, firing on all cylinders and forcing me to leap into action. In the wild, in a primitive setting, this would be helpful. I would immediately run from the impending predator and the primal responses learned from my hirsute ancestors would probably save my stupid life. In a domestic setting, adrenalin generally works against your best interests.

I leap up, catching the back of my nightie in the ball of my foot and for a minute I am Wile E. Coyote on the edge of a cliff. Arms spinning wildly, face a cartoon mixture of fear and comic confusion. This is appropriate, because the window-cleaner is grinning placidly and simply watching, much as the Road Runner would have done.

Eventually the Earth's spin and gravity's insistence requires that I fall backwards, missing the piss-filled potty, and land with my nightie floating upward in slow-motion and my fanny clearly visible to any window-cleaning Fred Quimby creation who might unexpectedly look through the window.

I sit still for a moment, waiting for the boulder I was trying to push on top of the Road Runner to land on top of my own head. When it doesn't, I can safely assume that I am in reality, and I peep through my bare knees. The window-cleaner waves.

'Hello love! Thank you for that!' He shouts cheerfully.

I wave back enthusiastically.

'Hello!' I shout through my open legs. Even flat on my back with my fanny in the air and my elbow in a recently-used potty — recently used BY ME — I am nothing if not British. Bloody hell, I wouldn't want to be RUDE. It might offend somebody.

Still, I don't come away from the incident entirely unaffected. I'm still pissing a lot, my skin looks great, but I'm going to buy a pair of pyjamas.

I get the kids dressed and take them to the charity shop for something made of affordable cotton which an old man has probably died in.

Life is sometimes safer that way.

MUM AND DAD'S

I am at my Mum's for tea tonight.
I'm at my Mum's for tea most nights, my Mum and Dad being two of the only people whose company is actually any use when I'm with the children. It's a thankless task, being a parent. For me and for them. All those years they spent, trying to instil in me a sense of confidence and self-esteem that I might leave them and forge my own destiny in a cold and unforgiving world. Years creating a person who would be able to grow up and grow away and basically, I suppose, fuck off and leave them alone.
And here I am back here again every night, eating their food and filling their house with screaming kids.
Will I one day reward them with a huge and remarkable gift, a granny flat in their frail dotage perhaps?
Will I fuck. I love them but Christ, once I've got my strength back I've got my own life to live.
My Dad doesn't care. He knows that life treats you a bit shit, but he's chosen to let it make him laugh. Whenever I tell him any problem I've had, anything at all, he says,
'Your mother and I went through all that. We had that for seven years.'
Kids piss the bed? Won't eat properly? Keep beating the shit out of each other?
'Your mother and I went through all that. We had that for seven years. Seven years of it!'
Then he laughs so much his Adam's apple bobs up and

down and he nearly chokes on his ginger-nut.

'Only another twenty years of torture!' he says merrily, face deadpan, eyes lunatic.

'Twenty-five years until they bring their own kids round to your house and you have to start all over again!' and he lights a fag, chuckling to himself about how crap his life is and how crap everyone else's is going to be. My Dad is the only person in the world who can chuckle without actually smiling.

'What are you doing?' asks Mum. She's talking to me. Probably because I'm hunched over the patio with a piece of chalk, trying to draw circles around the ants.

'Rescue him! Rescue him!' shout the children, presumably as an incitement to ant fervour in the rescuing department. Mum looks confused, but she frowns when she's confused so she just looks a bit pissed off. She's not pissed off, but you'd have to know her really well to know that.

'If you draw a chalk circle around an ant,' I sigh, as if everyone should have this information at their fingertips, 'eventually all the other ants in the colony come and rescue them.'

'Can't they just climb over it?'

'Ants can't climb over chalk,' I tell her confidently, the evidence of my own childhood shrinking away in my memory.

'Yes they can,' she points out, frowning. She's actually concentrating, she just frowns when she concentrates as well. She's looked pretty pissed off for the past thirty years but she's been either confused or concentrating for at least some of that time.

'Ant escape,' warns my oldest son, unintentionally making up the title of what could be a surreal animation voiced by Kurt Russell. I know, I know, I haven't changed. Neither, it would seem, have the ants. Maybe my life isn't that much fuller now.

'Who told you all this?' asks Dad. He speaks with gravitas, my Dad, he can't help it. When I reply I feel as if I'm giving vital information to do with German tank movements and positions held behind enemy lines.

'Mr Carey,' I say. 'That teacher I had in primary school.' Dad sucks his cigarette for the last time and stubs it out in the gravel behind the patio. He raises his eyebrows and draws his lips tight over his teeth in a grimace to show he has reservations about bollocks like this. But he likes that sort of thing, I know he does, and better still, it's INTERESTING FOR THE KIDS, so he approves.

'So who is this Ben person then?' asks Dad. I've been telling Mum about him, Dad was pretending not to be interested but obviously can't hold out any longer.

'Has he got a job?'

'Oh, for Christ's sake!'

My Dad grimaces again, I'm in the wrong, he knows it, but he doesn't give a shit. Caring about good jobs and money and security and pension plans is something that, even though I have kids, I still feel too young to start doing. His grimace says, 'You'll learn.'

It's funny how parents assess the worthiness of your potential sexual partners as a spirit level for the effectiveness of their parenting. The bubble stops in the middle for 'doctor' or 'lawyer'. 'Single mother', that's tipping the scales pretty dangerously, I think they want to even out the balance with a good sex match.

'We've got some flea powder, by the way,' says Dad. He's not that much of a lunatic, I did tell him about my flea problem. He doesn't just burst out with stuff like that.

I suddenly realise the fleas have gone.

'The fleas have gone,' I tell him. 'They've just gone.' My body has now been re-decorated by a couple who are a bit more up-market, they just did a single-colour wash and left it at that. Cheers. My body and my face are now smooth. I see my reflection in the patio door. I look okay. That's good enough. Hey, that's more than good enough, it's fantastic.

'It must have been the cold weather over the winter,' says Dad. Has it been winter? Oh yeah. Not any more, though. This warm snap should really bring those ants out.

I suppose you think I'm going to say that now I've got the smooth face and body that I wanted, I don't want it that much any more. That I've suddenly found something else to worry about. Not a bit of it, oh, reader of little faith. I am fucking ecstatic. I keep making 'Quantum Leap' jumps in my head — where I remember how I felt in the past and then imagine my past self suddenly being thrust into the present — and I feel amazing. My acne-ridden, tortured past self is the one who is looking in the patio door right now, not some smug, smoother, self-satisfied modern me. It's the old me, the acne me, the one who looks at her face and it makes her feel like Christmas day. Thank you, thank you, thank you so fucking much!

'Your spots have cleared up a bit,' says Mum, not realising the joyous tumult in my mind.

'Now I bet you find something else to bloody moan about.' My Mum goes inside to play patience really fast. Her mind works incredibly fast, and her nimble fingers show how her hand-to-eye co-ordination is in perfect harmony with the quickness of her brain. It's just a shame that she's chosen to become incredibly good at PATIENCE, for fuck's sake. It's not even a game you can win against someone else.

So much energy, where's it all going? Dad really should get her a treadmill or something.

She picks up the ball for the dog, and chucks it through the open patio doors. It dribbles listlessly into their garden but the dog is ecstatic. A moving ball! A moving ball! All her primal urges, everything her ancestors ever wanted her to do are satisfied by chasing that small moving sphere. Chase it! Grab it! Take it somewhere! She's got it all sorted out. Sure, things are calling to her from the past, but its stuff she can pretty much handle.

'My back's fucking killing me,' Mum says. She loves that crappy little dog, she does, but you'd have to know her really well to be able to tell that.

'Is there dog poo on the lawn?' I ask, wondering about the children contracting not an ant rescue service, but toxoplasmosis.

'No. The bloody dog's constipated. She hasn't done a shit for a week,' Mum tells me.

'She's on the way out,' says Mum cheerfully. 'Aren't you baby?' she rubs the dog's ears affectionately, as if she hadn't just been talking about her impending death.

Bugger.

I'd bought my Mum a little comedy present for her birthday, nothing expensive, they hate that, just a present to show I know them well. I'd got her a pooper scooper.

It seems a bit, well, tactless to give it to her now.

I suddenly need to do something meaningful, something with a foreseeable end and a resolution. Something with a fucking POINT.

I go outside and help my Dad with the chalk circles.

So this, this drawing chalk circles round ants on concrete, this is the fantastical tale of childhood I have for my children. Not that I'm complaining or anything, I mean, a lot of a story is in the telling. And ants are a whole world in and of themselves, children know that better than anyone.

I'm trying to make myself feel better about my crap contribution toward the 'tales of childhood' situation, because my Mum is actually telling the kids a story.

They've given up on the ants — just one more of life's failed expectations. To cheer them up, Mum is telling them a story about her past. It's one I've never heard before. Isn't that ironic? All your childhood, you're waiting for your Mum and Dad to do the Roald Dahl bit, or the Enid Blyton bit, sit you on their knee and regale you on a winter's evening with wild stories from the murky past. At the time, they seemed more interested in getting you into bed early so they can argue about the price of re-covering the sofa while watching 'Panorama'. You have to wait until your own kids are born, that's when they've actually recovered the strength to become the fully-rounded individuals they were before you were born, I guess.

And wasn't Enid Blyton supposed to be a shit mother? Don't sue me for God's sake, I read it somewhere. She was so busy writing stories about perfect childhoods, she forgot to give her kids one. Maybe I'll stick with hearing Panorama through the walls of my gerbil-infested bedroom, at least I knew they were there.

Anyway, Mum's got this ship in a bottle. It's been there for fucking years, getting more and more yellow and repulsive, but now I know how she got it. She watched the bloke making it when she was seven, just after the war, on a boat from England to Africa. Africa, for fuck's sake! She watched a ship-in-a-bottle maker plying his delicate

craft on a boat to Africa and I only hear about this now? Then she moves on to the story of the black mamba (she's presumably managed to get to Africa by this point, either that or it was one fucking hell of a day at London Zoo). The black mamba wove between her legs down the garden path, then legged it into her house where it ate her new kitten.
She's only had dogs ever since.
I am rapt, captivated by the story like....like someone watching some ants rescuing each other. I look at the boys.
They don't give a shit. I grimace at them, and my grimace says 'you'll learn'.
Christ, after all that excitement, Chucky Egg must seem like a relief.
If my Mum favours the weaving of technicolour glory in her childhood tale technique, Dad is the opposite. They say that everything wasn't really in black and white back then, it was only the photographs, but just ask my Dad. It was. But then, to a stubborn realist like Dad, everything in life is monochrome, he's not the embellishing type.
His stories include little Johnny something-or-other, who had his whole face burned off and is a lesson to us all about putting coffee cups in the middle of tables. And what about the time a little dog followed him home and he wasn't allowed to keep it?
Even now, poor bastard, he's married to a woman who despises the sight of his naked feet so his whole life has never been what you'd call particularly easy.
I think about my Dad wanting that little dog sometimes, and I want to get my kids something wonderful, let them have something amazing to kind of make it up to a little boy in the fifties who never got his dream.

'Let's get a rabbit!' I say, 'a kitten! A hamster! Anything, anything you want guys. Let's do it!'
'Nah, me no like annamal. Me want train,' they say.
Bastards.
My great-grandfather was always in the pub. He wasn't INTERESTED IN THE KIDS, so my grandpa decided to make sure he would always be the father that he had always wanted. I think this explains my Dad quite a bit, his father was pretty hands-on for that day and age, hence the INTEREST IN THE KIDS my Dad always thinks that men should show. Yeah, it makes sense. And the fucker had one HELL of a jawbone. I think it was him that started the whole thing off. No, really, you could hang your laundry off that bloke's chin.
He wouldn't have done the whole ant thing, though. He would've been in the pub.
Mum and Dad both had Great Danes when they were kids, a strange coincidence, but it has resulted
in the fact that now they obviously just don't feel comfortable unless their whole house is dominated by enormous animals needing to shit. They met at a party which is probably just as well, because Christ knows what Mum's lonely heart's ad would've looked like. 'Uptight smoker with secret passion for unusual pets that shit a lot seeks similar to start family. Ability to clean shit essential, no bare feet please. Big jaw bones only need apply.'
The kids are going to Tone's tonight, so I have to get them home.
Dad stubs out his fag with a manly urgency, the kind of urgency that once hurled itself over trench- climbing ladders, and stuffs in a ginger nut. Mum kisses the children and Dad drives me home.

I get back to find Gemma's room empty, empty except for one box.
She's gone. She didn't even say goodbye.
Now I feel fucking guilty.

SATURDAY

It's saturday, remember? The party?
Well, I'm going to it. It seems weird for Gemma to just suddenly move all her stuff out. I mean, I know we talked about her moving out but I thought she'd give me a date or something. She's so fucking weird. I can't believe she's missed her final opportunity to say 'see YA' in that knowing way that winds me up so much. Oh, just once more for old time's sake. Tone is coming any minute, so I brace myself for the smell. I know I've got a life of my own now, I don't have to be jealous of him mingling aromas with teenage tarts, he can mingle away.
I am still a bit jealous. The smell in my house is mine alone, well, if the kids haven't pissed the bed or crapped on the lino during the past half hour. Sort of mine, then. Me mixed with piss. Nice.
So I'm still a little bit jealous.
But I'm going to a party, and when he comes in I gulp down the past two years and smile at him.
He looks surprised.
'Goin' out?' he says.
'Yup. The boys have had tea. Do you need clean pants?' I deliberately don't specify who the pants are for, just to see if he's up for lightening up the mood between us.
'Nah, I 'ad a bath this morning,' He almost, almost smiles at me. Almost. The liberation of not FUCKING HATING another human being fills me with joy like a helium

balloon. Hatred is like lead in the guts, it weighs you down.

'Phone me if there are problems,' I say, normally. Just being normal is amazing, like a whole new me. I can be normal with Tone! This opens up all sorts of possibilities, like not having my innards churning with seething disgust and fury everytime the fucker knocks on my door. I'm going to set myself free.

Tone picks up the youngest toddler, golden autumnal toddler, and carries him out to the car.

I'm free now, really really free.

Five minutes later and I'm running to the station, panting and laughing. I feel exhilarated, Christ, all this from a story about a black mamba and not minding a smell. Not quite.

Ben phoned me last night.

It's his party.

Here's the bastard thing about it, though; Ben is moving away. He's going to live in Manchester, because he's got a job animating a children's programme, and if you've got to live in Manchester, that's a good reason, I guess. This doesn't make me feel as bereft as you might think. I don't know, maybe you're not thinking too much about this at all. Maybe you don't give a shit, who knows, but I do because I am bloody here, right here in the action.

I feel okay about it because most of our friendship is conducted over the telephone anyway.

Also, I know I shouldn't feel bereft about it because I am supposed to be in love with someone else.

I AM in love with someone else, it's just that my someone else doesn't slot into the kid jigsaw quite so easily. I'd have to sand down a fuck of a lot of his reservations and his

preferences for doing his
music first, even then he'd probably have to be rubbed down with industrial swarfega to crow bar him into my life. He just doesn't fit.
Ben loves kids.
He likes MY kids.
Shit, I've met the man of my dreams six months after getting hold of the man of my dreams. What a mess.
Danny meets me at Brighton station and we drive to the restaurant in his smelly, tinny car. We're having dinner with Ben and all his friends first, then going back to Ben's for the party.
'Ben says you were on the phone with him for an hour last night,' says Danny, without a hint of suspicion. I feel guilty. I wish Ben would cover the tracks of our friendship furtively. Like the bastard that I secretly am, I think of our friendship as an unconsummated love affair. Fuck, what else could it be, you mad fucking hippy? I don't say this out loud, partly because I don't want to offend Danny, but mainly to save my own skin.
'I'm so glad you get on with my friends, sweetheart.' Danny smiles at me a little bit sadly. I get the feeling he wishes that everything else between us wasn't quite so fucking good. The sex, the parties, the friends. He wishes I didn't have kids. He does.
I don't wish that, in case you're wondering. Not even for a minute. It would be like wishing I didn't have ears. The kids are a part of me, they came out of my body, they're supposed to be here.
The restaurant is one of those candle-lit Italian jobs, with huge mirrors all along the back wall. Two months ago, this would have been a nightmare. But then two months ago, I looked as if I had put my face in a blender and then

covered the shredded remains with heavy foundation. Now, I look okay. A bit skinny, yes. Flat-chested, I'll agree. The jaw isn't to everybody's taste and I cut my own hair. In fact, this dress is ten years old but it's a backless mini-dress in a size six, and the only item of clothing I have ever worn that makes me come close to feeling as if I am squeezed into it, in a womanly way. It hangs off my chest a bit now, but I still remember that feeling. I look okay.

Ben leaps up and hugs me tightly. He doesn't smell of anything.

'You look amazing! You are so beautiful I can't believe it!'

If he had whispered this into my ear, the game would well and truly be over. Fat ladies would be singing, chequered flags would be waving, and John McEnroe would fling down his tennis racket and storm off the court. Game, set and match.

But he doesn't.

He says it loudly, grinning from ear to ear. Christ, I love his grin. His small blue eyes assess the dress. It's for his benefit, sort of. Does he know that?

'Wow, that is a fantastic dress. Is that for my benefit?' He says this loudly, too, grinning at Danny who is standing behind me, ducking under light fixtures.

'Everything is for your benefit tonight, Ben. We pay homage to you.' This is Danny, who moves in to hug his friend, and I edge away a bit. I just can't judge this situation, what is going on? Can a man think you're beautiful, dream about you, talk with you for hours and still not want to fuck the living bastard arse off you? I mean, what is going ON here?

We all shuffle around, all the other Brightonites and Ben and Danny and me, all trying to secretly get to sit next to someone we like but trying not to make it look too obvious.

'I bagsy Elaine first!' shouts Ben, and slips his arm through mine.

'Sit next to me, gorgeous.' He tugs me down next to him and my face appears in the mirror opposite.

I look like a calculating bitch.

After the meal, we light cigarettes on the candles and talk in loud voices about sexual politics, the way drunk middle-class English people in restaurants often do. The lights go further down and the music goes further up. It is salsa music. I'm not just setting the scene for you there, you need to know what sort of music it is. Salsa music, okay?

Good.

Ben is rotating around the table, spending some of his precious last night with every person here. He migrated down to one end earlier in the evening, and is now gently coming in on the tide of people on the other side of the table. He is just about opposite me now.

I'm trying to analyse his motives for sitting next to me FIRST. Did he want to get it out of the way? Afterall, I'm the person who probably knows him the least well in this whole restaurant. Apart from the waiter, and to be honest they look as if they're getting on pretty well now, too. Have I mis-judged this whole thing?

If I have mis-judged it, I deserve the disappointment. I'm a calculating bitch.

Suddenly, Ben notices the music.

'Music!' he shouts, not inaccurately. Then he does one of the single most romantic things anyone has ever done for me. This is one of those moments, right now. Put on some salsa music, go on, put some on and really think about it.

He stands up and in one swift and graceful movement he leaps right over the table, placing one foot next to the burning candle and nearly setting fire to his trousers. It is a bound, a real bound, not something you see every day. Ben is a big man, he's not tall but he's big. The type that ping pongs between stocky and chubby depending on life style. I don't mind chubby, who fucking cares about chubby? Not long ago I was pebble-dashed, and I expected people to look beyond it. Ben is the sort of chubby that looks like big shoulders in the right sort of shirt, and I hate men with skinny legs anyway. Big men moving gracefully is a breathtaking feat of nature, like elephants swimming, or lions hunting. I am spellbound. I am, I'm fucking spellbound.

Then he is standing next to me and taking my hand and spinning me round. Not round and round like your Dad used to do when you were a kid, holding both hands and making a wide circle with your fingers in the epicentre, not that. That would be silly. No, I mean he properly spins me — spinning as in salsa dancing, as in twirly skirts flying up on hot Cuban night.

Then we are dancing round the restaurant, and I mean properly dancing. Not that crap drunken torso bouncing that knocks over furniture, but properly dancing. He is an amazing dancer — fluid, graceful, sexual, and everyone stops eating to watch.

I love dancing. I love anything to do with sex and believe me, if you don't think dancing has anything to do with sex, you can't dance.

It is Romeo and Juliet reciting perfect poetry at first meeting, it is Maria and Tony singing in harmony without any practice at all. This my friends, was a partnership waiting to happen.

'I took salsa lessons while I was unemployed' he grins at me. Then quietly, in my ear, 'everyone is watching us.'

Yeah, that's pretty furtive. Game, set and match.

We stop dancing when the music ends, we don't drag it on and bump into tables and start getting on people's nerves. It was the perfect moment, and perfect moments end like that. Just that.

When we stop, he holds my hands and kisses me lightly on the lips and the restaurant breaks into rapturous applause. Danny stands up, clapping and laughing.

'You are so lovely,' he says when I sit down. 'That was fantastic.'

I look at his face, and find it full of joy. Then he asks me to cut off my own ears. Well, not quite. What he actually says is:

'If you didn't have kids, I'd marry you tomorrow.'

BEN'S FLAT

Ben's flat is a twenty minute walk through night-time brighton. I love the smell of cities at night, if the adjective 'exciting' had a smell, this would be it. 'Sadness' would smell like the perfume you were wearing when you broke up with the love of your life, and 'holiday' would smell like the inside of a wooden chest of drawers. Chests of drawers on holiday always have that fresh woody smell, every time you put your pants away your senses spring into life with joy.

Never mind all that now, we're walking through the streets of a night-time city and I think we've both heard the clichés before. The shiny streets, the harsh glare of the street lamps, shall I just cut to the chase?

Ben's flat is big. This is a good thing, because there are bloody hundreds of people here. I don't mind being in a bustling room full of happy, free and childless people if I can pretend I am one of them. Hello, hello, yes yes, well, I have two kids, yes it IS very fulfilling, especially on my night off. Ha ha, yes I'm very friendly and sociable aren't I, you bunch of childless happy carefree cunts. I know that's unkind, I know there are good people among them, they have chosen a happy carefree life and who could blame them?

I'm jealous, sometimes, I can't help it. I told you I was going to be honest and I am.

I'm jealous of them.

I'm wearing a lot of make-up, that's something else I can't help now. Like the fat person who loses a lot of weight and can't stop going into fat people's clothes shops. They just can't believe it. All that anxiety, it never quite goes away.
'You're wearing a lot of make-up sweetheart,' Danny tells me. No shit. 'It makes your face look sort of.....flat.'
Flat I can handle, sweetheart. It was the agonising boils I had a problem with.
'I can't stop putting it on,' I tell him. 'I put a bit on, then when that looks better I think, well, if a bit looks better, then surely loads and loads will look better still.....'
'It doesn't work like that. You're bonkers.' Danny kisses my forehead, but he does mean it. The bonkers thing, he really means that.
'Are you talking about Elaine's make-up?' asks Phil. She is here too, she loves parties.
'You look pretty and everything, it just looks too flat. It needs some shading.' Shading my face, what am I, a charcoal sketch? 'You just slap it on without thinking about it. A few weeks ago, that girl Jo saw you and asked 'who's plastic face?'. I told her you were my friend and stuff but, well.....she's got a point.'
Plastic face. Here's a phrase to burrow down into your core and take root. It'll find fertile ground amongst the compost of my self-esteem. Plastic face. Fucking plastic face? I try to conceal my irritation.
'Plastic face? That's a fucking rich stone to throw from the glass house of fucking ugly cunt.'
Danny and Phil exchange a look, they put up with my vulgarities, my outbursts. But I catch the look.
Sometimes my verbal front is a downfall for me. It gives the impression of a barricade, of strength and resilience. Really, of course, it is just a desperate attempt to prop up

my personality, lest it should crumble inwards and reveal itself for the shabby self-doubting whimpering little creature it is.

I can see where Jo is coming from, though. You make assumptions, don't you? I can see how she saw me — bleached hair, loads of make-up, a large and vulgar mouth saying loud and vulgar things. Not nasty things, not that, Christ I wouldn't want to offend anybody, but just generally sort of...loud and vulgar. It's a persona I've cooked up to conceal my social inadequacies, but you'd have to know me pretty well to know that.

She doesn't know about the acne, the pain, the poison-filled pebble-dashing and the general misery my face has forced me to endure for the past two years. How could she know? She looked at me, saw a heavily made-up blonde, and considered me fair game. For the first time in years, I have been out in public feeling okay. Nothing adventurous, just okay. That's all I wanted to feel. That I had a face like most other people's faces, nothing special, just okay.

Plastic face.

Shit, that's unkind.

I wander through the flat, getting drawn into conversation here and there with various attractive and intelligent people, such are Ben's many friends. We hug, exclaim, laugh and pass comment. It's a party, for God's sake. Picture it.

Danny is talking to Fifi. I don't mind this, I'm not really that jealous, but he looks pretty happy
about it. She's funny, Fifi. She's making him laugh, which is nice isn't it?

Do I sound jealous? Maybe I am a bit.

She's a bit like me, in a way. Sort of skinny, sort of funny, but she hasn't got any kids. A better version of me, then. I feel like the donkey on Clacton peer to her Red Rum. I hope to Christ Danny doesn't think that too. I am a bit jealous.

I end up in Ben's bedroom, where people sit and stand and smoke and lounge. There are drugs here, recreational drugs taken by people who can afford them. There's no boarded-up windows or hollow- eyed addiction here, this is the drug-taking that nobody talks about.

Ben is lying on his bed, smiling up at me. He pats the duvet beside him.

Can you misinterpret someone patting a duvet? I wish he were a more obvious sort of man. Yes, enigma and intrigue are all very exciting, but it's starting to lose its charm. I was born in South London in nineteen seventy-three, the only enigma we knew about was a prostitute called Big Bertha who used to ply her trade down the end of our road.

I don't make much of a hippy.

I lie down next to Ben and rest my head on my arms, looking up at him. I'm quite conscious that this sort of activity will make my compressed ear go bright red, but I try to look carefree. It's a party, for God's sake. Ben and I start to talk, to talk and talk, the people around us coming and going like one of those speeded-up films of city traffic they do on the telly. We are the static core, the epicentre, the eye of the storm. We don't move at all.

Then Ben stops talking. His eyes assess me, accurately. Small blue intelligent eyes, dotted with freckles.

'I love you.' Is all he says.

I am caught in the stillness of the moment. I am on the inside, snug and warm.

'I love you too.' I say. I kiss the pale freckles on his

outstretched arm.
Fuck.
This could be a problem.

What does 'I love you' mean to a hippy? I'll tell you what it means to me.

He loves kids.
He's a good cook.
He's a fantastic dancer.
I get the feeling all I have to do is to pull out a garden centre leaflet from my pocket and we'll be as one. Here is a man who will visit bogs and ducks. Gasp with wonder at a giant carp. The tiny worlds in the gaps between the world are his and mine, our own private crappy Narnia.
Just squeeze the fucking thing, just fucking do it.
The acne has gone, but here is a new problem: Danny. I can't believe this. My problems have swapped seats.
Christ, I'm an ungrateful bitch.

Out in the hallway, later on, I see Fifi with her arms around a man. Any bloody man, I don't care who it is, it's not Danny, that's the thing. I feel like I've scored a point over him, but I don't know what it is.

On the walk back to Danny's house we have our first row. I am anxious about being drunk, about it being six o'clock in the morning, about having a hangover when the kids come home. I can't cope very well when I don't feel well, and Danny's idea of a good night out usually involves not feeling very well in the morning.
We've left the party now, and I am a Mum again. A drunken, staggering Mum, about to snatch a few hour's

sleep with the curtains closed against the sun. That's not nice. I feel dirty and horrible, a bad example, a nasty piece of work. Tone will be at my house with the kids in twelve hours, I have to recover by then. The old fear is seeping in; I can't cope, I can't cope, and I did it to myself.
They deserve better than me. I hate myself.
Danny is irritated by this, he wants me to be carefree, like his life is.
'You always do this.' He says. 'You always get pissed then spend the whole weekend worrying about it. Why can't you just relax and enjoy it? You always have to spoil things.'
His tone is petulant. I've spoiled the night. It's the 'you always' that kills me; he's never said that before. We've never had a row before, never brought up little nuggets of bitterness from our secret misdemeanour tally. He's not calling me 'sweetheart' now, not now I've let my anxious, inadequate self intrude on his party night.
This is the first blip on the seismograph, the darkening of a summer sky. The weather is changing. When we get to his house I sleep on the sofa downstairs. I've never done this before either; our time together is too precious and fleeting to be wasted. But I'm not thinking about Danny now, I'm not thinking about Ben. I'm thinking about two little boys missing their mummy, a mummy who has made herself too ill to look after them. Mummy is passing out on the sofa, what sort of mummy is that? A shit one.
I hate myself.

IT'S OVER

It's the next morning. It's midday, actually, but in the world of hangovers this one has definitely been seduced by the White Witch and is currently giving some evil wolves the exact location of Beavers Dam. It's an evil one, sapping the life out of me. I smoke a fag and feel about a million times worse, like I knew I would. Danny comes downstairs in his red dressing gown, looking like an upper crust debaucher. He sits next to me.
'I'm sorry sweetheart,' he says sadly. He kisses me on the lips.
'I'm sorry too,' I say. I mean it, I can't bear this sadness. I want everything to be okay. I wanted Ben until it occurred to me that having Ben would mean losing Danny.
'We have to talk,' Danny tells me. If he didn't think that would ring alarm bells, he's not as insightful as he thinks he is. The bells are ringing so loudly I think for a moment that I have developed a sudden and severe case of tinnitus, until I remember that I have a hangover. Fred Quimby birds fly tweeting around my head, and Tom sneaks up behind me to bang two dustbin lids together. Surprise!
I didn't expect to have this conversation, not this morning.
'Talk about what?' I ask him, but I already know. I just want to be wrong.
'Can I come round tonight?' he asks, and for a moment my

heart leaps with joy. Then he says, 'I want to talk to you when you feel better. After the kids have gone to bed.'
Right.
He wants to say something that I need to feel better to cope with, something he doesn't want the kids around for. He's going to end it.
'You're going to end it, aren't you?' I say. I am caught again in the stillness of the moment, but not in a good way. The world holds its breath and waits for the answer. The talking trees stop waving their arms around and incline their heads towards us. Always winter and never Christmas, that's the story of my fucking life.
'I could keep you hanging on for years, enjoying being with you, enjoying the sex,' he begins, and I am so still I can see my heartbeat under my shirt. ' I can't do that to you. Oh God.' He hangs his head down, looking at his knees. They don't help, they're just patellas.
'This is the hardest thing I've ever fucking done,' he tells me. Yeah, try having kids mate.
I look at his head, his black hair, his long brown neck.
'It's over, sweetness.'
The spell is broken. It's all broken. How can somebody save you only to throw you back? I don't give a shit about Ben any more, only Danny. My beautiful olive-faced wolvine man, my sweetness and my saviour. Come back to me you fucker.
I am running around the room, shaking my hands at the wrists. I always do this in times of crisis, I want to shake the badness from my hands, hoping it will simply slide right down and plop out onto the floor.
'It's not over! It's not over!' I am crying now, the stillness is gone and so is Danny. Not actually gone, not yet. He's still here, looking at me with tears in his eyes.

'Don't make it harder, please. I don't know how I can do this.'

'Don't fucking do it then! Take it back!' I beg him. Oh God, I'm so shit. I really really beg him.

'Say its not over! Say it! Say it!' I fall into his arms, and we lie together sobbing with the curtains closed against the cruel day.

Somewhere in the world, a bird sings. But I don't hear it.

That was the love Kessel Run in twelve parsecs. Well, I told you it was quick. He really is a nice person, you know. If he wasn't, all this wouldn't matter, but he is.

The crying and the begging are finished now. We are sitting side by side, talking about it. It's different, this loss, to losing Tone. Tone was pretty brutal about it. He loved someone else, I had to fuck off.

But Danny is gentle.

'I thought I could handle going out with someone with kids,' he says, 'but I can't. I have to tell you that. I can't let you hold on forever, waiting for something that's never going to happen. It could be ten years before I'm ready.'

'I'd wait ten years for you.' I say quietly. I would, if I knew for sure it would happen.

'Oh, sweets.' Danny is crying now. Properly crying. He really does love me, how weird. How strange to feel more loved now, when we are breaking up, than I ever did when we were together.

'I'll never regret this year. It's been a wonderful year. It's given me back my confidence.' He is sincere, I can tell that. I think about what he just said. Yeah, its true. I'm a different person now, and that doesn't seem to be slipping away along with the tattered remains of our relationship. It was love when I needed to be loved. Now I'm stronger, I think.

I'm Peter and Susan, in book four when they are forever banished from Narnia. Its just not right for them any more, but they have found the strength to leave. I have the strength, too. I really do. I have been loved, held, heard words of tenderness when my shattered self was breaking.

Now I feel ready. Scrubbed down, straightened up, and made ready for the next round.

He is so gentle, my wolvine man.

His kind brown eyes are full of truth and innocence. Its like sobbing into a gentle dog's fur — they don't really understand you, they can't help you, but they know you're upset. They give what comfort they can. Any actual analysis they might have of your situation would be shit. Still, there is love there somehow.

We are a species apart, Danny and I. Parent and non-parent. It would never work, but the sex was great.

He drives me to the station and I catch the train home in the orange afternoon sun. When I get home I find Gemma leaving the house taking her final packing case, and two messages on my machine.

DAY OF THE PANTHER

I deal with Gemma first. She's moved out all of her stuff when I haven't been here, she hasn't even said a word about it. That IS weird, isn't it? This is a surreal kind of day, my life seems to be sloughing off bits of itself like a snake. Everything's falling away. Not in a bad way especially, but just sort of renewing itself.
Christ, when life decides to have a sort-out it really does chuck a lot of shit away.
I feel sad about Danny, but not as sad as I did. The kids will be home soon, I'd rather give up Danny for the kids than the other way around. Oh God, not the other way around. I feel virtuous now. I have made THE RIGHT CHOICE. After all the begging and the 'oh, don't leave me' stuff, obviously. It's going to be okay.
'Is that the last of your stuff?' I ask Gemma. She is walking past me with a box full of unidentifiable teenager-y things, little china animals, a hair drier, a picture of a faceless teenage moronic boyfriend in a heart-shaped frame.
'Yeah.' She says. Needlessly, really, it's certainly not mine. I don't even brush my hair, let alone sand blast it dry. I can't stand women who fuss with their hair, it's dead, leave that shit alone.

'Well, I'll see you then,' I tell her, hoping I don't.
'See YA' she says, slyly, edging her way out of the door. Christ, don't drop it love, you need those china animals. Your next house would look SHIT without them.
The back door slams shut. The house is empty.
Hang on, the house is MINE.
All mine, for the very first time. No Tone, No Gemma, it's all mine, like my life. I feel sloughed, shaken up, refreshed and made new. I'm doing the right fucking thing, in my own fucking house, and I feel good. I don't often do things like this, but I put my arms in the air and whoop loudly like a teenage pop fan. It feels great. Gemma has gone, no more wondering, no more guilt, just gone.
I face the window, looking out towards the day. Arms raised I whoop and whoop with my fists clenched in joyous salute to new life.
'WWHHHHOOOOO — oh, back again?'
Gemma has come back quietly through the back door and is watching me expressionlessly from the doorway. She walks upstairs. I half-expect her to barricade herself into the bedroom and shoot at me through tiny holes she's bored through the ceiling, but she doesn't. She's coming back again.
She gives me one last look as she descends the staircase, clutching a hamster cage with something perched on top. A book perched on top. Oh, it's her diary.
I hold the door open for her this time, having broken into her room and ransacked her belongings and celebrated her departure, I feel it's the least I could do. She doesn't look at me, she just walks out, parting more central than ever. I close the door.
'See YA,' I say. Quietly.

After five minutes of sitting quietly in my house, MY house, I feel guilty. The secret phone-calls, that was all in my head, wasn't it? She wouldn't have moved into my house just to keep tabs on me for Eva. Fuck, this isn't Nazi Germany, people don't infiltrate stuff anymore, we're all friends now. No-one would ever bring Eva into my house. No-one who'd seen me try to kill myself would bring that business back into the house. No, I'm a mad paranoid arse-hole.
I phone her. I'll invite her round for a drink, just to show her that there's no hard feelings.
I'm so weak. Last week I was desperate for her to fuck off, now I feel guilty. I just wish she could have fucked off with a smile on her face.
She doesn't answer her phone, I'll phone her later.
I am just about to check my messages when the phone rings. This is one of those rings, this is someone's life changing with one single ring. Can you hear it? Ring ring. Ring ring.
'Hello?'
'Hello? Is that Elaine Kirby?'
'Yes.' I don't like this. No good news uses your surname, well, hardly ever.
'We didn't know each other very well, but I'm Robert.'
He's absolutely right, we can't ever have known each other very well because I haven't got a bloody clue who he is.
'Robert.....' I try to combine not knowing with a sense that I'm bound to remember, so as not to offend him.
'I lived with John.'
John?
John! My friend John! Christ, I MUST phone John, I really

must phone him.

'I'm afiaid John died yesterday morning. I know you were good friends and I found your phone number in his book.' I feel ice cold. I never knew that someone could die before. Not someone you knew.

'How did he die?' I ask. I want to know, so I ask.

'He had throat cancer. He didn't want to tell anybody, or make a fuss, even at the end. That was John.'

……..hang on, I remember Robert now.

'Weren't you living with John?' I ask 'When your mother' — shit, I need a good euphemism — something fucking sincere and inoffensive — 'passed away? You lived with him, didn't you'.

'For about thirty years, yes.'

Robert sounds a bit prim about what he must know is a bombshell for me. A bit 'how could you not have known? We dared not speak our name' about it. But it's not my fault, I wouldn't have cared. I wouldn't have fucking cared, John, you idiot. I wouldn't have fucking cared less.

'Thirty years?' I repeat, just because my throat is no longer producing enough saliva for sentences. 'Yes. The funeral is next week.' I feel frightened of bereavement, I've never been close to it. Not in adult life.

I know I won't go, but I write down the details anyway. John is dead. I must phone John. You can't, you idiot, he's bloody dead.

I sit in my house and listen to Robert's message on my machine. Shit, I'm glad I was on my own for that one. I am crying again, my eyes are stinging from all this salt, but I can't stop.

Shit, shit, shit.

I never phoned him.

Well, I'll never make that mistake again.
I get up and put my trainers on and pat some powder over my sticky cheeks. My hair looks a mess, but it always looks a mess so I feel okay about it. I light a fag and lock the back door, my back door, to my own house, where I can make as big a mess of my life as I want.
But not today.
I still have four hours until the kids come home, that's long enough. I never phoned him, I never phoned him.
I start trotting at what your Dad would describe as a fair pace towards the station.
I never phoned him. Shit, shit, shit.

I'm going to squeeze the fucking thing. I'm gonna tell him, I'm gonna fucking do it.

There are twenty minutes until the next train to Brighton, so I lean against the ticket machine and try to look lost in thought. Station platforms are great places to people watch, but they can also be great places to be shouted at by aggressive people who take exception to being stared at. This one isn't too bad, big posters for West End shows starring people who left soap operas for Hollywood but never made it. Adverts for books about spies with flames coming up over the author's name. It's just a platform.
Then I remember that John is dead, and my tonsils feel too big inside my mouth. I was his friend, and I didn't even know he was dying, what sort of friend is that? The sort that doesn't bother to ring for years on end. The sort that didn't even know he was gay.
Just what sort of person am I? I thought I was good, relatively.

Danny is gone, John is gone, Gemma is gone, maybe it's me, maybe I can't hold on to anyone.

A man in his twenties walks past with a skateboard and long shorts which hang past his knees. There is a lot of that around here, boys seem to grow up slower down here near the south coast. Maybe it's the money, maybe it's the climate, there's nothing to propel them into maturity unless they get their girlfiiend pregnant.

My resolve is starting to wither now, all the losses of the day are welling up in my eyes and I think about going home. I could watch a funny video. I want to take my head off and scrape it out.

I hear the clang clang clang of stupid shoes on the metal staircase behind me. It's that time in the evening, the very first stupid shoes are making their inevitable way down to the pubs and clubs of Brighton.

The stupid shoes are accompanied by chattery voices, stupid chattery voices, the sort of voices that chatter and chatter and never say anything. They're off to the bright lights where nobody will be interested in what they've got to say anyway. Clang clang clang, oh get on with it.

The chatter stops suddenly, and the clanging reverses.

Clang, clang, clang, up the stairs now, what the hell are they doing, those stupid bloody clanging clattering girls, don't they want to have a meaningless encounter with a moron tonight?

It takes a minute to dawn on me, what has happened.

The clanging and the clatter, that was all going fine for them until they got to the bottom of the stairs. They saw something which made them go into fast reverse, and the only thing at the bottom of these stairs is me. Unless you count the poster for 'Day of the Panther' by Overexcited Schoolboy, with flames licking

his dramatically embossed name.
I go to the bottom of the stairs, and look up. Three fat arses are going upwards in a hurry, all tight mini skirts and blotchy legs. Straight hair, flat to the head like a cartoon waiter and three centre partings all in a row.
It can't be, I can't believe it.
Two of the heads swivel round and goggle at me, and for a second I am staring into Eva's eyes for the first time since she ruined my life.
The other pair of eyes look at me without expression, like they did the last time they saw me. It's Gemma.
My first emotion is so huge I don't know what it is. Then I start to narrow it down. Anger, yes, that's in there. Betrayal, I feel a bit of that too. Fuckers. That was my home, and I wasn't safe in it. Mainly, and this is hard to admit, but mainly I feel embarrassed. Embarrassed that it's all been such a cock-up, that I couldn't even live out the simplest human life span without screwing things up. But I was right. I'm not bloody mad, or paranoid, or any of that stuff. I was right!
Gemma looks at Eva and I feel as if I am seeing her for the first time.
She giggles. She does, she bloody giggles. I've hardly ever even seen her smile.
All her gravitas, all that solemnity, that was for herself.
'I'm grave and solemn because I'm concealing emotions far deeper than you could ever imagine,' her manner seemed to say. 'I am tortured by demons which make me a REALLY INTERESTING PERSON...okay?'
But this tragedy of someone else's life, this only makes her giggle. I am watching her observe the betrayal and misery of my own life, and it makes her giggle.
Now I'm sorry I was nice to her when her granddad died.

He was old, get over it. People die every day, sweetheart. Hey, that puts me in the mood for a bit of a giggle. Now I'm sorry I only read her diary, I wish I'd crapped in her knicker drawer and opened her post as well.

Actually I already did one of those, this afternoon after she left, but it was just the results of her smear test. She's not getting them now, she and her fanny can fuck right off.

The adrenalin is starting to do me some favours.

It's like a kick up the arse from fate, almost. As if fate is saying 'Come on! You ARE right about some things! Don't give up now you stupid fucking cow!'

I am right, I've certainly got more insight into human behaviour than the Day of the fucking Panther. I'm going to do it, I really am.

The train pulls into the station with an obscene sigh like a fat person coming. I get on and find a seat that hasn't got a discarded Metro on it and sit down, noticing that somebody has left their greasy head stain on the window. My mind, ever the fourteen-year-old, is suddenly distracted from it's inner turmoil and revels in the disgusting. My good side loves a moral dilemma and I ponder the next one all the way to Brighton.

'Would you lick that for a million pounds?'

LOVE, PART I

Brighton is only twenty minutes from our town, but it is like a different country. Everyone in Brighton looks different in order to look different from everyone else, hence the fact that everyone looks the same.

Brightly coloured slightly bedraggled gypsy skirts and dreadlocks litter the station. I have to squeeze gently past a couple with matching red mohicans and a couple of toddlers with hand-knitted jumpers just to get to the ticket gate. I like it, though, its like a carnival every day. There're no judgements here, you can look as scruffy as you like.

I put my hand up and ruffle the back of my hair a bit, just to look the part. I catch a cab to Ben's flat, wondering all the way if I should make conversation with the cab driver. I don't feel too guilty today, my head is too full of other stuff.

Like death and loss and betrayal and stuff like that.

Ben isn't at his flat.

'He's at the Green Goblin,' says his flatmate, smiling at me. He's a good-looking hippy, that bloke.

'I'll come with you, shall I?'

'Er....yeah, okay,' I say. I don't know quite what to do now. In Brighton people do this a lot, pop in, pop out, yeah hey cool whatever man. I can't do that. I like to make arrangements. This is out of character for me, and Ben will know that, and he'll want to know why.

Oh, shit.

'So.....are you up for chilling out later?' says Ben's hippy friend. Fortunately I've been to this country before, I speak fluent hippy.

'That would be so cool, but I have to go home and get some head space before the kids get back,' I say. The kindly hippy nods wisely. Head space, and the having of it, is important to Brightoners. I have hit the right note.

'Well, lets just stay chilled for a bit together.' He says. 'If you're cool with that.'

'Totally,' I say, smiling back. He's smiling, for God's sake, don't be so cynical. I told you I was weak for kindness.

Ben is indeed in the Green Goblin, which is a pub painted green. He stands up to greet me with a hug.

'Hello beautiful! Amazing to see you!' His smile is massive, a whole room of a smile, and his small intelligent eyes spot me hiding something big.

He doesn't ask me about it, he just looks at me closely, then sits down again. He resumes his animated conversation and I feel suddenly lost and stupid. What the shit am I doing, chasing round Brighton after chubby men I hardly know?

I'm about to slip out the way I came, when Ben beckons me towards him. 'Come here.' He leads me by the hand towards the back of the pub, through the tangle of dreadlocks and young people all being vastly different to everything except each other.

'I do need to talk to you, actually.' He says, and pulls me into a little alcove between the pub and the back door. We are screened off in here, the coloured lights in the door reflect in his glasses and I think, if Jesus had been chubby and born in the seventies, he might have looked like that. His Yorkshire accent gets me every time. The way he says 'come' with an 'oh' sound instead of an 'uh' sound, that gets me. Christ, I even like his vowel pronunciation.

'I came down to talk to YOU,' I say. I can't look at him.

'Just tell him! Just fucking do it!' screams my good side. It has been following the story like a hawk, and like a normally decent person watching a gangster movie, it is completely caught up in the action.

'I fancy you,' I blurt out, what a twat. 'Fancy'? What am I, twelve?

Ben doesn't say anything. Then,

'Don't lay this shit on me Elaine.'

What? Whatever else I expected him to say, this is not it. I expected him, at the very least, to turn me down gently. This is another hammer in the tonsils for me today. Shit, I feel like I've swallowed a hedgehog and rubbed my eyes in roll-on-deodorant. The physical effects of misery can be a source of misery in themselves.

'Don't....don't you fancy me?' Oh, stop it. Stop it. Stop seizing the fucking day, you stupid cow. It worked for Robin Williams, but not for you. Just stop.

'Don't you? I thought you did. All the presents and the party and stuff …… ..'

I can't let it go now. I'm a terrier for love, I can't let it go until it's dead. Sometimes they play dead just to get me off.

Ben is quiet now, he can't look at me either.

'I don't fancy you.'

'Oh.'

That's that then. Go home, shoot yourself, no harm done. Game set and match. 'I wanted to talk to you because I knew how you felt. I've known for ages. I'm sorry.' He looks sorry. 'So that's what you wanted to say? Just no thank you?' I feel embarrassed again. Like I'm such a

nuisance, such a randy terrier, it needs a special 'will you just fuck off' speech to deal with it.
I feel ashamed, exposed as being randy and unwanted.
'I'm gay.'
Pardon?
'I'm gay.'
That was Ben talking. His blue eyes look frightened behind his glasses, he suddenly looks about fourteen. He looks embarrassed.
We are silent for about fourteen seconds, then I say the words I've been needing to say all night, words that have been eating through the hull of my soul. Wherever, whenever he dies, he'll have heard this first.
'Do you still love me?' He asks, he really asks me. He means love him properly, not fancy him, he's asking for acceptance, for approval. This time, I can do it, I can really fucking do it.
'Ben, you idiot, I don't care. I couldn't fucking care less.' I throw my arms around him and we stay like that for long minutes, warm in the stillness of the moment, the eye of the storm, the epicentre of
our love. I feel forgiven.
Ben and I are sitting side by side, holding hands under the table. This is both more and less that I was expecting. He squeezes my fingers and kisses my cheek, and I feel warmed up as chicken soup. 'You're the first person I've ever told,' he tells me quietly. 'I always thought something awful would happen if I ever said those words, now I wish I'd said them sooner.'
'You're not the only one', I reply, but I'm joking. I don't mind. He's had bloody big fish to fry. 'So all those presents and stuff, all that telling me you love me, you actually do love me? You weren't trying to shag me at all?' Ben shakes

his head.

'I just love you, that's all. Nothing personal, I'd shag you if I could, but the thought makes me feel a bit sick.' Yeah, cheers. If I still had acne that would cut me to my battered core.

'So I've finally met a man who genuinely loves me for who I am.'

Ben laughs at this.

'To be honest, I thought you must all know. I hate football, I love cooking and dancing. Christ, how many clues do you need?'

'I didn't think you were gay. I thought you were the perfect man.'

We don't stop holding hands until it's time for me to go. The kids are coming home soon.

I kiss him goodbye, on the cheek, and take a deep breath. He smells of nothing, nothing at all. Maybe a gay man's smell is like a dog whistle, only other gay men can smell it.

'I'll phone you soon,' says Ben. 'I'll want to talk your ear off.'

I catch the train home in the orange evening sun, home to my home, home to my family.

It occurs to me that for the first time, I have heard a man promise to phone me and been absolutely sure that he means it.

Fuck, that's true love.

I look out at the fields and see they are festooned with daisies. Summer is coming.

LOVE, PART II

Oh, shut up. Don't tell me they're just weeds. The daisies, I mean. They're not weeds, not to anybody with half a soul anyway. You'll be telling me that foxes are vermin and squirrels are rodents next. Yeah, yeah. And snails are just slugs with portacabins, whatever.

Some people just can't wallow in the completely uncontrived mystical beauty of the world, can they?

So, here I am at home, one minute and twenty seconds before the boys are due back. I'm going to

give them coco-pops when they come in, keep them busy while I re-adjust back into mummy mode.

The phone rings.

Shit, I can't take any more revelations, not today. For the first time in my life I hope to God it is the phone company offering me some absurdly complex discount scheme.

'….and if you come over to us, we can offer you ten pence off every phone call made to somebody with an 'M' in their name every weekend that you're having your period.' I don't even know who my suppliers are for anything any more, they're always at my door, demanding my loyalty to their offers to save me TEN POUNDS A YEAR. The bloke with the clipboard always has this look as if he's saying, 'you'd be a CUNT not to do it, you really would,' so I do it. Now I think I've got about twenty gas suppliers all fighting over the privilege of serving me discount energy.

Anyway, the phone is still ringing, whatever discount schemes I have I still have to answer it.

It's Steve.

'Hello Steve'

'Hello. Can I come over tomorrow? I'm...er...going out with Emma again.' Emma is Steve's girlfriend, who I've yet to meet. 'I want you to meet her this time. Don't worry, I've told her you're a cunt.' He says this cheerfully as ever, but I feel like a sunflower under a sledgehammer.

'Do you really think that?'

'What?'

'That I'm a cunt. Do you really think I am? Sometimes I think I might actually be one.' Steve is silent. He's known me long enough to know when there's a subtext. He waits for it, I can almost hear him pushing his glasses up his nose.

'John's dead,' I say.

'Oh God.'

He doesn't need to say anything else. He knew John, too. 'Am I really a cunt? I never phoned him, Steve. Maybe I am. Sometimes I wonder if you even like me when you say that'.

Me and Steve's friendship is based primarily on banter, but that's about to change.

'You think I don't like you?' Steve sounds genuinely surprised. He seems to realise that something is different today, all this loss, this sloughing off, I feel worn out. Locusts are easiest to eat just after they've sloughed their skins. They're softer.

His tone becomes something I've never heard in Steve before. Gentleness.

'I don't like you eh?' he says. Then tenderly, 'Elaine. Don't be a cunt.'

Wow. It really is a term of endearment.

Tone is here, shit, he's at the door. I don't mind, I feel papered over, polyfilla-ed and sanded down. I'm not perfect, but I'm okay.
Feeling loved armours me. Yeah, yeah, make what you will of my self-esteem. I can cope without being loved, but at this point in my life, I am, and it feels great.
I open the door and smile at Tone. This takes him aback, I don't smile at him that much.
The kids storm into the house, more noise and movement than one adult could ever make. Tone gives me a plastic bag, chocolate from his Mum.
As I take it our fingers touch, the first time we have touched since he ruined my life. I breathe in.
He smells okay.

Later that night, Phil comes round and sits quietly while I cry and cry. Not hysterical crying, I've still got all my hair by the time I've finished, and I actually feel better. Phil doesn't stare at me while I cry, but she doesn't look away either. She doesn't pretend she's even more upset than me, to get a notch up on the 'emotional and interesting' scale, but she does share it. She doesn't tell me it doesn't matter, but she doesn't blow it out of all proportion. She's perfect.
'Your kids still bore me,' she says. Okay, she's not perfect. But she's pretty good.
I laugh. She's so inappropriate it makes me laugh. I run my hands over the corduroy and feel it flatten and ruffle under my fingers.
'You'll have kids one day,' I tell her through my tears, like an overly emotional fortune teller. She's quiet for a

minute. I think she's having important thoughts, so I let her take her time.

'They're not as interesting as taking drugs and having sex with people,' she says bluntly, as if this is going to come as a surprise. 'But your house is full of.....'

'Shit?'

'No.'

'Lego?'

'Not that.'

'Screaming, tedious, boring arsing bloody children?'

'....that as well.'

'As well as WHAT?'

Phil takes a fag out of the packet and puts it in her mouth. She looks at me and for a minute I bless her honesty. I know whatever comes out of that mouth will be what is inside her head, I can't wait to hear it. Come on Phil, do your worst, you can't be any more offensive than you have been on every other occasion I can think of. Go for it. Spit it out.

She doesn't break my gaze for a second.

'Love,' she says.

FAST CAR

That was all two weeks ago, I still can't believe it. Everything just exploded on one day, but I feel alright, I really do. Just in case you were worried about me or something.
I've cried about John quite a lot during these past two weeks, but it's not any kind of desperate grieving emptiness. Sadness happens, I'm dealing with it better these days.
I've talked to Ben a lot as well, he phones me nearly every day. He's working up to telling his family he's gay, and I'm supporting him. Yeah, I really am, and I feel good about it. There's no 'dare not speak it's name' stuff going on between us, I'm helping somebody. I know quite a lot about feeling like shit, you may have noticed. The good thing about it is that now people who feel like shit like talking to me. Christ, the past. It's like a skewer sometimes. But at least my friends know that we're all jammed helplessly onto the same kebab.
Danny phones me, too. We've written to each other about our FEELINGS, maybe hippies do have the right idea. I don't feel severed and bereft by all this loss, I'm doing okay.
My parents are here at the moment, fussing about the dog crap in the garden. They came round to pick up some jelly bowls that they left here last week. Mum makes jelly for the kids, and makes them guess the flavours before

they eat it. This would be less sinister if I did not get the impression that she does this to my Dad as well.

'Get some bloody bog roll for God's sake before Elaine sees it,' says Mum, quite loudly for somebody who is attempting to conceal a shit.

Dad comes into the kitchen and looks under my sink. It's right there, he knows my house.

'Has the dog crapped in the garden?' I ask.

'No,' says Dad, innocently. He comes back in a moment later with a turd wrapped in toilet paper and flushes it down the toilet. 'Just pretend you didn't see it,' he says.

The boys clamour for his attention while he washes his hands.

'Hold on boys, granddad's just cleaned up the doggy do-do,' says Dad in answer to their grasping fingers. Impressing on their tiny minds the importance of having an animal in the house that always needs to shit, and thereby continuing the family madness for the next generation. Mum comes in and gets them to pick up the dog ball for her. 'Gran can't bend down that far any more,' she tells them. 'Do you know,' she says to me, 'I can't even do a hand stand these days? I'm so fucking old.'

'Mum, you're sixty two. Of course you can't do handstands.'

'I can do what I bloody well like.' My Mum sticks out her lip like a child, making me feel suddenly protective of her. She's mad, my Mum, but she's got spirit.

'So,' she becomes my Mum again, and forgets about the handstands, 'have you got my bowls?'

I feel sheepish now, because I've lost those bloody bowls.

I look in a few cupboards, just for effect, but they won't be in there. Some saucepans fall out.

'Why don't you arrange them in size order?' asks Mum.

'Then they wouldn't fall over when you open the door.'
Because then I'd be YOU, Mum.

'I can't find them,' I explain, I'm nothing if not honest. But Mum's face is staring into the garden in disbelief, her face a picture of horror which I know she's doing mainly for effect.

'I can see one now, and it's IN USE!' she exclaims, pointing. 'Those bowls belonged to nannie James!'. Nanny James is another relative of mine with a jaw-bone you could use to plane down planks of wood. Get a spirit level on that woman's face — that's flush that is.

I follow the direction of my Mum's gaze until my eyes come to rest upon my guinea-pigs. In their run. In the corner of the run is a small bowl, which is filled with water. Actually, it is half-filled with water and guinea-pig shit, but I can see that it was probably quite a nice bowl at some point. That point being before Mum gave it to me.

Her gaze swivels round and she points to the second missing bowl. It now holds about twelve used tea-bags and is stained brown like a fake Da Vinci. How did I manage that? It's been an emotional few weeks, I haven't been concentrating on receptacles.

My Dad bustles her out by the elbow before her outrage can manifest itself verbally, ruffling the boy's hair on his way to the door.

'Don't worry about the bowls,' he says, 'Nanny James had about twenty of those bloody things,' and he helps my speechless mother up the garden.

'Next time,' I just catch him saying to Mum, 'next time, for God's sake just get her some from the pound shop.'

To make it up to Mum, I buy her a present. I don't often buy her stuff, so she'll be pleased. I've put some thought into this one, and I'm quite proud of myself. I seem to be doing things right at the moment.

They're back again, delivering more jelly in cheap bowls, and I give it to her. I've even wrapped it up. She looks genuinely excited, the plus side of having a child-like personality. Small things make her laugh and excite her, it's only adult life that makes her look a bit pissed off.

She sits on my sofa, all wrinkles over high cheekbones, and examines the gift.

It is long, like a serving spoon with a large spherical bit on one end, I'm really proud of this one. Guess what it is, go on. It's perfect.

'Oooooo! What is it? What is it?' she says, laughing with excitement.

'Elaine's got you a bog brush,' says my Dad, drily.

The children crowd round her to watch, they are excited too, even though they know what it is.

'It not a train,' says my eldest, solemnly preparing her for the inevitable disappointment that this discovery will invariably provoke.

It's not a train, it's better than that.

She pulls the paper off carefully, storing it away so it can be put away to be used again. Not actually used again, you understand, just put away in case the need should arise. Mum was born during the war as well.

It's open now. You want to know what it is, don't you? I'll tell you. 'What IS it?' asks my Mum, wielding it about a bit, as if practising for a sport she is never going to master.

'It's a ball-throwing thing, Mum. You know, for the dog. You don't have to bend down to pick up the ball any more. You scoop up the ball with that bit, and just sort of …...lob it. It's twangy. It lobs it miles.'

Mum stares at it for a bit, and then starts to laugh. Not full-on, sharing-the-joke laughter, but laughing as if she knows it's not really funny. Something is going on. She points at the dog.

I hadn't really looked at the dog until this point, I must admit. Now I look at it properly. It's a medium-sized black and white thing, like a big jack russel with a sweepy tail, but she looks different today. She's walking slowly round in a circle with her head bent over at an angle, mournful eyes gazing up beseechingly. Christ, that must be a big shit. Either that or.....

'She's had a stroke,' explains Mum. 'She can't run any more. Not in a straight line, anyway.'

'So she can't get the ball?'

'I think it's blinded her. She can't even see the bloody ball'.

There is silence for a moment. Then, one by one, we all start to laugh. Nervously, at first, as if nobody wants to admit it, but it builds up. Then we are helpless, tears in our eyes, passing around the ball-throwing thing as if it were the golden idol from Indiana Jones. The first movie, you know, the good one with Marion in it.

We're not laughing at the dog, we love that crappy little dog. We're laughing at life, at what a cock-up it all is, we're laughing at each other, at everything. The kids join in, even though they don't understand, they're just caught up in the action.

Even my Dad is laughing, a proper wide-mouthed laugh which is echoed in his eyes. He's letting his hair down, but gingerly. Go on Dad, spend all your laugh rations in one go for God's sake. All his gravitas, all his solemnity, he was keeping this all in check.

Gemma's giggling was the opposite, somehow — the revealing of her true self was less like letting her hair down, and more like ripping her wig off to reveal a bald and blistered scalp. She's a Roald Dahl baddie in my head, now. In my mind, school boys with mice in their pockets look on in horror as she reveals herself for the bastard she is. But let's not dwell on her.

Mum is laughing more than anyone, like I told you, she only sweats the small stuff. This, this real life tragi-comedy, this only makes her laugh. Like the time a boyfriend of mine walked into the patio door and smashed it, costing thousands of pounds and losing them their no-claims bonus. My

Mum pissed herself over that one.

'When did it happen? Why didn't you TELL me?' I ask, when we have calmed down a bit.

'A few weeks ago' says Mum, 'We left a message on your machine.'

Oh, right. That was the second message. After the one about John dying of cancer, I didn't want to listen to any more. I didn't think reality had any more to offer me, I just erased it.

Sorry, dog.

'Never mind,' says Mum, and she doesn't mind, I can tell. 'Look what we made, me and your Dad.' 'Mum's got a new hobby,' says Dad, his eyes crinkling slightly, which is Dad's version of a broad smile.

Really? Is it another unproductive exercise which requires excessive clacking?

'We've been weaving!' This is unexpected.

Mum holds up a large, hand-woven rug. It is beautiful, absolutely beautiful, and I can't believe it. 'You MADE that?'

'Yup. Your father's made a wooden loom, it's in the garage.' My Dad looks proud, as if he has planed it down using only the firmness of his own Adam's apple. And who knows? He probably has.

I look closely at the rug, it looks oddly familiar.

'What did you make it out of?' I ask. Mum almost hugs herself with excitement.

'My old duvets!' she says happily, 'Your father's been ripping up all our old duvet covers and converting them into rugs! Look, look at this one, do you recognise it? It's the one Monday had her puppies on thirty years ago, I was up all night washing out the afterbirth.'

Monday was my parents' first beseeching dog. That one not only shat a lot, it also gave birth. She lived for about fifty million years then just sort of faded away into the past.

Now, it would seem, she's back. In rug form.

Fuck, that is one resonating rug. That is a rug with a story. But it is beautiful.

'And look at this!' Mum brings out a photograph. 'I found it yesterday. Look at the size of that dog!'

The picture is of my grandmother, you can tell by the jawbone. She looks like the kind of woman whose grandchild would use a family heirloom as a guinea-pig's water bowl. I can't believe it. She's

got a great big beseeching bastard bloody dog. Is the whole family on weird pet auto pilot?

'That's Bruce, the great-dane,' says Mum. Nanny looks young in the picture, well, as young as anybody could look in those days. She looks pretty happy about the dog.

The last thing Mum presses into my hands from her bag are two jellies, for the kids, wrapped in cling-film. Mum points at the bowls. She looks a bit pissed off again, but I don't think she is, I think she's just thinking.

'From the pound shop,' she says, pointedly.

It occurs to me then, all the clacking of my childhood, all the mind games, the patience, the Chucky Egg, that was my Mum's equivalent of bogs and ducks. That was her giant carp. She was creating alternative realities for herself, tiny moments outside time, when the constant demands for Sindy accessories seemed to be driving her over the fucking edge.

My Mum is a Mum, too. I realise this a little late, I think. I've been taking the piss for nearly thirty years.

She's me.

Now I've finally admitted this to myself, I can at least put my saucepans in size order in the

cupboard. It'll stop them falling out.

Two days later, I'm lying in bed with my arms around the boys. We've eaten our dog's fanny pasta, we've looked at the leaflet for the London Dungeon, we're pretty contented.

Yes, I know they've got their own room now, but sometimes I like to just taste the future before eating the whole thing. I like to balance on the precipice of possibility before taking that leap, just to enjoy the moment. And touching the boys is always like finding a lost part of myself, as if when they were born a part of me plopped out, and I've been searching for it ever since. Part of me doesn't want to let them go. I hug them, because I mean it.

There are no fewer than four home-made rugs on the floor.

The room looks like an Arabian brothel, but the boys don't know that. 'You got spot,' says my oldest.

'Yes darling.....' 'What that stuff on it?'

'Errm, just.....spot stuff, you know.'
'Mell minty. Mell toofpase.' Yeah, okay, I've got a spot. I put some toothpaste on it. So what? It's just a spot. It's not the end of the world.
I'm telling them about my plan. I've read, in a book, that rabbits can be trained to use litter trays like cats can. You can actually keep a rabbit in the house, like a little dog. That sounds so crazy, like the image of the fifties schoolboy with the mouse in his pocket, that I want to do it. I want to be a part of that crazy.
I've heard about giant rabbits you can get, bigger than cats, bigger than foxes, even. Great big bastard beseeching bloody rabbits. Christ, that sounds like a lot of shit. But fun. My brain is hot-wired to 'weird pet' auto pilot, I can't help it. It must be genetic. I'm trapped in the hamster-wheel of the past.
Christ, the past. It's like a skewer sometimes. But it's also a clay mould, it's the shape of me, the shape I am. I won't change.
Besides, I've never had a rabbit before.
I'm going to fill the house with life. I'm going to phone people the second I think of it. Starting now. Just squeeze the fucking thing, just fucking do it.
'What shall we call it?'
'Florence,' says my oldest, immediately.
'Why, darling?'
'No reason.'
No reason?
What, just pull a name out of no-where, no connections, no resonance? This has not occurred to me. A name, no reason. Just floating around in the name ether.
Christ, that's brave. My son isn't skewered on the past, his past is still to come. This is his first chalk mark on that

clean slate.
Let's do it.

I tip-toe downstairs, full of excitement. The kids are happy. I'm brimming over at the thought of this bloody rabbit, I'm bringing home the bogs and ducks. Hell, I'll even attribute unlikely human qualities to it, describe it as 'cheeky', really enjoy myself. Maybe I'll ditch the die-hard cynicism, the ruthless search for personal truth. Fuck it, I'll enforce a personality on that bloody rabbit. God knows I've had to do that with flatmates enough times.
I need music, a song about new beginnings, a poignant song about starting again, a clean slate. Ah, this is it. This is the one.
I put on 'Fast Car' three times in a row.
Old habits die hard.

What? Oh, that. Crumbs, you've got a good memory.
Okay, we've come this far together, I'll tell you. It was 'Some Mothers Do 'Ave 'Em.'
Funny, eh? Things never turn out the way you expect.

Printed in Great Britain
by Amazon